Daughters of Captain Cook

ALSO BY LINDA SPALDING

The Paper Wife

DAUGHTERS
OF CAPTAIN
COOK

LINDA SPALDING

THE ECCO PRESS

THE ECCO PRESS
100 West Broad Street
Hopewell, New Jersey 08525

Published simultaneously in Canada by
Penguin Books Canada Ltd., Ontario
Printed in the United States of America

Published by arrangement with Birch Lane Press,
Carol Publishing

Library of Congress Cataloging-in-Publication Data
Spalding, Linda.
Daughters of Captain Cook / by Linda Spalding.—
1st Ecco pbk. ed.
p.   cm.
ISBN 0-88001-551-9 (paperback)
I. Title.
[PS3569.P3386D3   1997]
813'.54—dc21   97-16823

9 8 7 6 5 4 3 2 1

FIRST ECCO EDITION 1997

This book is for my daughters
—Esta and Kristin—

with love and thanks to my mother
—Edith—
and to Michael.

I would like to thank Louise Dennys,
Lora Carney, Stan Dragland, Daphne Marlatt,
Jean McKay, Warren Iwasa, and Anne Phelps.
I'm also grateful to Marjorie Sinclair Edel,
Sarah Collins Howes, Annetta Kinnicutt,
and Philip Spalding for help
with Hawaiian aspects of this story. And
I thank the Ontario Arts Council for support.

Where is the sea
that once solved the whole loneliness
of the midwest?

James Wright

Daughters of Captain Cook

ALBUM

In early June, on the kind of hot still night that brings the crickets
and cicadas out in force, in a car polished until it reflects the
moonlight like a dark mirror carried under the open sky, my
grandparents float through dim Kansas streets.

My grandfather, whose name is William Tilson, sits at the
wheel peering out toward the almost flat horizon which, in the
new 1928 sedan, seems close and accessible for the first time.
He licks his upper lip and pumps the gas pedal a little, furtively
testing the energy stored there with his toe. The engine pulses in
the same way that the crickets and cicadas do, and William hums
along.

My grandmother is sitting next to him rigidly balanced against
upholstery. Her name is Alice. When she turns to look back at
my father, a small boy perched alone on the vast contours of the
back seat, she moves daintily, turning her upper body from the
waist. "Don't you forget now Billy," she says to the boy. "You
sit still as a cat in there."

The car, passing carefully measured elms that line the street,
stirs leaves and gives the faint impression of a breeze. Leaning
out the open window, Billy takes a deep breath of the sweet
grass smell that is the background of all his future memories.
There's something out there in that heavy sweetness he can

1

almost touch, something tangible that's almost within reach, and he is searching for it with his nostrils open like an animal's as he rides through the empty streets.

My father and his parents are on their way to the Chautauqua in Garfield Park where the night before they heard Lucille Elmore, ventriloquist, and Judge Kenesaw Mountain Landis, headliner. The park has been home to these gatherings off and on since the summer of 1887, when they were billed as An Intellectual Feast of the Highest Order, and A Fortnight in the Wood with the Muses. In those days, tents used to appear up and down Topeka's streets: Wilder, Vincent, and Topeka Boulevard; and they were occupied by prominent families from all over eastern Kansas. This year my grandparents have purchased season tickets for the first time. They've made the long drive in from Everest.

The car slows down and comes to rest against a curb. Climbing out, they hear the last of "Day Is Dying in the West", and Alice squeezes Billy's hand. Mr. Ray Jerome Baker, famous photographer who has been out to the Pacific Ocean, is going to show a travel film.

The big brown tent, lit from within like a soft canvas lantern, mounted on its wooden platform, is almost full. Alice and William find three seats together near the front, between two sets of uncrossed knees. "I've been among them now for more than ten years," explains Baker as Alice reaches up to remove her hat. "Recording the indigenous society."

Ray Jerome Baker is as Midwestern as anyone in the hall. But he has followed Edison's advice and moved out to Hawaii, recording with persistent tenderness what Edison calls a dying race.

Alice's new hat is on her lap and she is wondering if Billy can see anything between the shoulders up in front of him. The hat, like the new car, is the result of a prosperity that will disappear long before Billy or his parents can think of any use for it, or locate any need.

"We didn't mind the old depression all that much," Billy will say later as a grown man. "We lost the land and sold the lakes but everybody else was poor along with us. It wasn't a big shake. You got to see how little all that counted."

Alice sighs, pats her hair tentatively, and focuses for the first time on the illuminated screen, where an old man's long thin arm pounds something in a narrow trough.

"The dietary mainstay of the native race," Baker narrates, "is a sour pudding extracted from the taro bulb. This fellow accomplishing the simple act of food preparation is typical of the Hawaiian Type."

Behind the pounding arm a grass hut absorbs sunlight and a dog scratches his ear. In the shade of a sloping roof of thatch, a woman gestures crudely. She spits and turns away from the photographer. From his breast pocket Baker pulls a handkerchief and mops the edges of his face. "They don't like the camera," he concedes softly, as if admitting to a small and unimportant sin. "But what you see here are the last of them, the last of the true Hawaiian race...."

Moist where the wooden chair is pressed against her back, Alice twists in her cotton dress, carefully folds the program into equal parts, and fans herself. Even while she folds, her eyes are fastened on the screen where people arrive from upper right to join a feast laid out on mats at lower left. The women are on horseback and they carry wooden bowls of food dangling in nets. Handsome and dark, erect and proud, around their shoulders they wear strings of flowers, and the horses' manes are braided and festooned with flowers too. The women dismount in long dark skirts and high-necked blouses and arrange themselves in circles on the ground. A small stringed instrument is being played. What the boy sees and what his father sees is the long hair of women wearing flowers—the long dark hair of girls who wear no shoes and walk in necklaces of flowers.

3

What Alice sees is food. It's arranged carefully, a bouquet of pigs and vegetables and fruits and yams. Sitting around mats on the ground, guests lean against each other casually: mothers with babies, grandparents, and children thrusting bare toes from their awkward clothes. An elder standing near them moves his lips, perhaps in prayer.

"A Typical Native Feast," Baker announces. "A feast like this," he adds, "was prepared by the Queen for the world-famous writer Robert Louis Stevenson when he visited the island. I have actual photographs of the event. The clothes, the ukelele, and the prayers show Western influence of course. You can't escape it. Missionaries have been out there for over sixty years. Things have changed. People have died of measles and a loss of pride."

Displaying the American solution, Baker shows his audience the fields of cane, the little train, the mill, the lovely new hotel, its narrow pier, the almost empty, perfect beach.

"I took this from an outrigger canoe," he says. "Some of these boats are huge, hollowed from great enormous logs, and fitted with masts and sails for voyaging long distances. Some are built long and thin for speed." Through the shoulders in front of him Billy sees a long canoe perched like a spider on a wave, its outrigger a set of arms. Inside, men work in unison, paddling fiercely, stroking the boat up giant waves and down the inner curl of them.

One long, connected intake of breath is audible across the room as the scene shifts to flowers. Baker names them by families: heliconias from the bananas, the arum family, the orchid. The bright acanthus and the fragile ginger are his favorites. Adding reality to the amazing blossoms, a Kansas June bug beats its wings against the promise of the screen, and William grips his child's hand, bewildered by the lavish, wasted growth.

"Now," Baker says as proudly as if announcing an award, "you'll glimpse the miracle of paradise—a flower that grows disguised as a plain, long-limbed common cactus, saving itself

4

night after night until a summer night like this when, like a visitation, buds appear along its bumpy branches and open right before your eyes into these sudden, waxy, deep-cupped flowers, beautiful and fragrant. Brave as anything on earth."

The audience inhales again. Ray Jerome Baker has caught the blossom in its act of bloom, demonstrating the wonders of time-lapse photography and paradise at the same time. The June bug, frantic with longing now, throws itself futilely against the screen.

"The night-blooming cereus grows on a coral wall around Punahou school where it was planted by a missionary teacher who received it from a lovesick sea captain. It opens like this only once, then fades away, leaving bare stalks after the flowers fall."

On the vast lawn behind the wall, girls in white dresses move elaborately. They move in rows. They lift their arms and dance and flowers spill from their shoulders as they move and from their hair and from their hands and from their clothes.

Billy will think of the moth sometimes and the girls and the boats. But he will forget about the flowers until he's flown to Honolulu on his way home from the war. "And a girl came to meet us," he'll tell his daughter happily, "wearing a flower behind her ear."

"We'll bid aloha to them now," says Baker fondly, gallantly, as Billy looks one last time at the girls whose long hair and long clothing have been hung with flowers too remarkable, too foreign, to have fragrances he can imagine. In an effort to conjure up all that unknown, he leans back suddenly in his wooden seat in the tent and squeezes shut his eyes. And when he opens them, he sees the perfect accolade being offered, the Chautauqua salute, a fervent waving of white handkerchiefs begun in 1877 when it was apparent to the audience that a deaf-mute from London, Ontario, who had described Christ stilling the tempest in sign language could not appreciate applause. Since then, the signal of enthusiasm has been handkerchiefs.

5

The lights come on, and while some squares of cotton still wave in the air the pictures fade and Billy finds his foothold on the flatness of the aisle.

Alice, exchanging remarks with someone whose Christian name she wouldn't think to use, tucks her hair back and then replaces her new hat. William stands by impatiently, looking down at his polished shoes.

But Billy hurries up the aisle to step outside. In front of him, the town is one-dimensional. The street could be a set, with walls that interrupt black, empty space. The linden trees and elms in Garfield Park are still. The car is parked against a curb. Nothing moves. Perhaps nothing ever will. The year is 1928 and everyone in the Midwest is dreaming, still innocent, holding off prediction for as long as possible, believing life is lived between horizons visible from upstairs windows.

Anticipating an emerging warmth of flesh, the air has cooled, and when the tent flaps are thrown back neighbors come out into it like storm clouds in expanding and contracting shapes. Yellow light pours from the tent and everything in its arc is held and defined and protected against the darkness.

But Billy is no longer there. Blinking his eyes and paddling the air, he has moved off into the moonlit night. He is no longer there.

ONE

The day was like most days in paradise in June.

In the shadow of Diamond Head, under the ancient dark, hard cloud of crater and beyond the bright hotels and travelers, a boat was tacking toward the beach. There was a trade wind blowing in from the northeast—a sailing wind—the boat moving with it to the shore where a small crowd was gathering, while two of us, mother and child, played in the sea.

The child was lovely, sun-baked brown and radiant, her seven-year-old body slipping like a sea creature through the transparent waves as she kept the land and the ocean, the mother and the father, the floater and the sailor in view.

The father waved at her, tapping the sail that rose in a white triangle behind his head and grinning as she disappeared into the water and emerged again feet first.

The mother rode on the waves, watching and perfectly content. She floated on her back, as bodiless as it was possible for her to be, as the boat landed with a soft thud on the sand, announcing Paul's return.

The flapping sail, huge overhead now, beat furiously in the wind, the shadow of the crater lengthening as the sun fell away from it across the ocean.

"Jess, I need your help with this.... Kit?" Paul was behind the sail, unsnapping it, wanting me to understand, to appreciate, and to participate in this event. He was making a point. The boat was new, but he already had every line of her by heart. He had memorized her as a man would memorize a new lover's flesh and voice. The boat was going to be moved across the island that very day, that very afternoon, across the mountains to the windward side, to the estate Paul's family had owned until his father died. It was going to be moved behind our car on a trailer to Revere. Paul had decided this, brushing aside my arguments. The place belonged to the Hawaiian woman, Mihana, now. It had been left to her in Paul's father's will, and it seemed foolish— even dangerous—to tamper with it in this childish way, although I was drawn to it too.

The place is still known as Revere, after some township in New England that was the home of his missionary great-grandfather. The missionaries started arriving in the 1830s, from New England and New York. They came in groups on brigantines—and by the time they came, the ancient religion had vanished anyhow. Strict social hierarchies and rules, enforced by *kapus* or tabus, had been abandoned by King Kamehameha's son. But the missionaries knew exactly how to fill the gap. They taught the Hawaiians melody. They gave them hymns. They gave them the Bible in Hawaiian. They gave them their own written language. They taught them about industry and modesty and private ownership and Christ. They divided up the land. They were a close, Christian society. Even now descendants are called cousins, even Paul who'd been away so long.

In high school I saw pictures of Revere in a travel magazine. Once beautiful and grand, it looked, even in the pictures, wild and overgrown, and almost uninhabited. I cut the pictures out and stored them in a box under my bed. I was fifteen or so and Paul would have been gone from Revere by then, sent away to school on the mainland. And for a long time after I met Paul, I didn't make the connection between the contents of that box and the furious desire I felt for him.

Now Paul measured my resistance to the move across the mountains against his passion for Revere. The terms of old Hilton Quill's will were clear. The estate had been left to Mihana, the Hawaiian girl Hilton had raised, while Paul, to all intents disinherited, received only an allowance that compensated for the money he never made as a photographer. Healthy enough for us to live on, to be sure, but by the same terms we could lose even that if Paul tried to interfere with the running of Revere. But Paul wanted to sail his boat up and down the shore of his childhood. He wanted to look from the water through the trees and up to the old house. "The boat'll be closer to us there," he said, attracted to Revere more by genetic instinct than by intelligence, as if he thought our only proper destination was the past, as if we were still looking for a home. But for the last time, on that last, perfect afternoon, Paul felt me hold the twin hulls of our brand new Hobie Cat inside the waves of Waikiki, in present time, where things made sense and where I wanted to believe we both belonged.

When he jumped down and dragged the boat up on the sand, Kit and I were still swimming slowly, rolling and floating under the sky. Summer was beginning. The day was ending. A plane swam overhead.

Then Kit and I washed up on the sand and she scrambled onto her land legs and ran to help.

"What about Mihana?" I said for the tenth or eleventh time, when the sail was rolled against the boom and Paul was pushing the boat backward to the water again, leaving a trail of twin lines on the sand. "You'll be interfering with the *a'ina* or whatever she calls it, you'll be bothering the balance, you'll be.... Your father didn't want you over there and why should she?" My voice was swallowed by a crowd of helpers congealing on the shore.

Paul didn't answer. He was moving off toward the car, getting in and backing it to a ramp and sinking our trailer into the water where Kit and I with the help of the gathered crowd could guide the boat onto its metal flanks.

Then we sat together in the hot front seat, still in our wet suits, our gear behind us with the cooler, and the helpers waving us away. Paul opened a beer, knocking the cap off against the window ledge, and ran the cold bottle across his face. "It'll be okay," he muttered, behind the dark glass. "Trust me, Jess. And keep your eye on the trailer," he said, glancing back a last time to check the lashings and balance in secret fear that the whole thing might capsize in the middle of the Pali highway. "It was my mother's place," he said tightly. "Mihana won't care."

It was characteristic of Paul to persist in his own view of things. In his photographs, mountains lean into the earth as if they are imperiled by gravity. Trees brood. The ocean, lying flat on outcropping rocks, smothers the shore. All nature is compressed. My face is flattened and expressionless. Wide-angled, I have the dull look of an outcast.

Squeezed in beside our daughter, Kit, between her skin, hot and scratchy from the sand, and the hard metal fixtures of the car door, I turned to look back at the boat through the rear window. The late afternoon sun was turning dust particles into mica on the glass. Cast in that golden light, we hesitated for a moment while everything around us—the thin, steep mountains, the sea, the cars winding around Kapiolani Park—seemed to be caught in the moment with us. The old, opulent Outrigger Canoe Club was behind us as we drove away, part of an older, more gracious Waikiki. Paul could remember, as a child, swimming there. He ground the gears and we jolted off the curb into the street away from Diamond Head. My view of it was obscured by the dusty window and the yellow and pink branches of shower trees that hung like sprays of confetti, carefully spaced, along the way.

After a long swallow of beer, Paul gripped the bottle between his dark thighs, and ran a hand through his hair. Sun-baked, we were tired, and the edges of the day were beginning to meet at the back of my mind. Kit was leaning against me. Her skin was sticking to me; I could feel the sweat of it running down my arm and side, forming a map in the sand and salt, the three of us dragging a boat, lurching across an island in the late afternoon heat. But then, I thought, we've all been at this crazy lurch for generations. I'm set in the mold of my pioneer ancestors. I have the woebegone face of my grandmother, with her thin Midwest lips and down-slanted eyes. I see her in the mirror; I see her in Kit, who's already walking on the woman legs I saw around me in my childhood—long thighs, long, narrow feet. She could be resting in the doorway of a sod house. We repeat the footsteps of our ancestors. Paul too. He makes no bones about his own line of descent. He is a missionary son, returned.

TWO

How did we arrive at that sweet blemished place?

When your ancestral memory trails back across a continent like a long, drawn-out string knotted with events, with names on charts and tombstones from eastern America to the Midwest, with destinations reached and names of states, when you trace your path along it to this place, this set of characters, and these occurrences, you wonder if what happens is predictable, if it is anything but fate. My people have been nomads, always moving, planting themselves inside new scenery and changing it—leaving it ruined sometimes, or enriched. Paul's people must have been the same. This is our Anglo-Saxon heritage.

My great-great-grandfather came out to Kansas in a covered wagon, like so many others, from Virginia, with his sons and a brown bear and a tired wife who died one unacceptably hot day along the trail. He had an urge to travel and a call that must have come up in his blood, because when he caught sight of the Kaw River in full flood he jumped out of his wagon to the muddy bank, so full of admiration that he took a woman standing there along with him, a stranger he had never seen before, to be his wife. Together they took the swollen water in their stride and, with the wagon bearing all the weight of a new household, hands clutching the wooden rail of a ferry and heads high, they looked across and rode the river safely to the other side.

They claimed a section of land straight on three edges, shaggy on the fourth where it was bordered by the river, and, before the barn was built, they set his sons to damming up whatever water it could bring to that dry land. He wanted water and more water. He made lakes on top of his rich farmland as if he had an unquenchable thirst. And he filled the land with fish.

The other side, my mother's clan, came with the railroads. Seeing ahead of them the untamed, and furious at its emptiness, they built their towns along the tracks. Tough-bellied, stern, small towns—some of them are still there. My people remade the prairies, wrapping the land around themselves and changing its surface in a generation.

When I came along, the Kilmer paper announced the fact with pride. In this small town, even my baptism was news. I wore a silk dress made from my father's parachute. I was three years old and he was home from the war. He'd been a correspondent, according to my mother, although his articles weren't published in the local paper. But after he stayed home with us for a while he took off again. My mother said his work had called him back on the road. She had grown up with travelers. Her family had run a five-bedroom hotel in Council Grove—that was a town right on the double wagon tracks of the old Sante Fe Trail. When the wagons stopped, the railroad came through and my mother was surrounded by itinerants. Even the doctor who had his own room in the hotel reported it as no fixed address. Then the war came. My mother saw a soldier now and then traveling through—one day she saw my father and that was enough. She knew what she wanted. She was a great one for waiting. But I spent my adolescence wanting to go after him.

When I eloped, there was a small write-up in the newspaper. That was all. Paul had no credentials then except for his father's money. He had driven into town one afternoon in his old car

14

to look around. He had a '52 Chevy and a borrowed dog and a camera. He was wearing cowboy boots and a blue work-shirt. He had no family and no background that anyone at home could understand.

Because while my forebears were busy lopping off chunks of land in the Midwestern heart of America, Paul's people had gone another tack, taking a mail boat around the Horn to find a foothold in the pagan Sandwich Islands. And I didn't guess, growing up so cautiously between my father's vanished shadow and the strong impression he'd left on my mother's mind, that after an undeclared courtship, after a decade spent on our own westward moves, after our romance, our elopement, and our wandering, we'd find these islands for ourselves, where it's so easy to feel held by circumstance.

Paul was counting on the charms of inheritance. He must have guessed, as I did not, where we would land.

Once we were there, we rented a small house close to Revere underneath a mango tree and from our bed watched as its leaves, elegant and long, gleamed after a rain and swayed restlessly above us. Under this tree we were protected from sun and from the fierce tropical storms driven by trade winds that made our house resound with weather.

Around our place there was a tended garden—mock orange, plumeria, and heavy, fragrant vegetation, with the color of the yellow tree they call be-still, and the brilliant, varied bougainvillea, and the gaudy red flame of hibiscus covering the fence with silky veils.

Paul wanted to recover something lost, even if, in the process, we lost everything. Like all the unprinted negatives he kept in his room, the island, for Paul, was full of unseen possibilities; the island had significance for him. And we were pulling our new boat up the Pali highway, closing in on that uncertain claim.

I put my head back against the warm plastic-covered seat. I knew the ostensible reason we were moving the boat. "The races are about to start, aren't they?" I said into the heat. I pushed Kit in Paul's direction.

A season of races was upon us. Paul would need help.

I pictured us on the windward shore, the same people standing in a different light: I was stronger and more confident, I was sailing the boat. Mihana was on the shore, holding Kit's hand. Maya was watching too. They were watching me sail the boat to shore.

"I'll sail with you," I said. "You said you'd teach me how before the races start."

"Daddy, can we get some ice cream at the Chinese store?" Kit begged, tugging at him. "I'm hot."

Paul handed her his empty bottle and pointed back to the cooler. "Get Daddy a beer, will you, honey? And while you're in there, get yourself out a piece of ice to cool you off."

"But can we?"

I said, "Aren't they? The races? Who's going to crew?"

"Maya," he said. He had a lovely, lop-sided, foolish grin.

Mihana's daughter. Almost a daughter to us too. In the past year, since we'd arrived, she'd become Kit's best friend. She'd stayed with us dozens of times. With her peculiar grace, strong arms, hard-muscled legs, maybe she was a better fit than I could be. I said, "She's only fourteen...." I hadn't thought of her as old enough.

"You guys want to go up and take a look at the place where King Kamehameha pushed all the warrior guys over the Pali and conquered the islands and became king?" Kit asked for the hundredth time. She had been studying local history in the first grade at school.

Paul shook his head. "She'll be easy to teach."

"But Dad, I'm hungry," Kit whined. And her father, having drained his second bottle, promised her ice cream at the Chinese store. "No Pali today though. I don't want to pull the boat up that road."

16

"And Daddy you said I could get skates. When school got out. Remember? Remember that?"

"Remember that!" Paul mimicked, catching up with her.

"Jinx one two three four five six seven eight nine ten!" Kit roared. "Hey! You owe me a Coke!"

Maya knew the water, the boat; knew her own skill. Maybe she was the right one, I thought then. Maybe my disappointment was ill-timed.

Sometimes, after sailing at Waikiki, we drove home to the windward side the long way around the edge of the island, taking the beach road past Black Point and Koko Head and Hanauma Bay, enjoying the purpling light of the shore, past Fort Ruger, where the military let its officers relax next to a perfect beach that had once been, Paul said, choice Hawaiian land. Now the Hawaiians had been given housing lots close to the highway, far from the beach, one of those places called "Hawaiian Home Lands". We stopped, when we went that way, at Sandy Beach, where a truck at the side of the road sold manapua, steamy and hot to hold, a puff of dough with meat buried inside. If it was late enough, we ordered a whole plate of food — chili and rice or stew and rice with two scoops of macaroni salad for a dollar eighty-five. After a year here, we had a taste for local things, for manapua and plate-lunch.

But this time the late sunlight followed us up the Pali highway instead. Into the mountains, across the middle of the island and down, passing through the long tunnel without a word because it's bad luck to talk in them. Ahead of us was the windward plain and Kailua, our own town. Kailua is a small place — orderly and middle class, built up along the beach, and not very old— although there was a settlement here once long ago. It's called the bedroom of Honolulu now, a bedroom full of families and Marines. Once there were pastures and taro groves, an ancient *heiau* or temple called Ulupo, and, at the end of the beach, a jungle under a cliff. Now there are houses and churches and

17

stores. On one side Kailua stretches out into a thin finger of land between the beach cliffs and Waimanalo. That's where Revere is. In Lanikai. Our house is about two miles away, toward the Marine base, in a section of town that was reclaimed from the bay. The land there is flat and covered with coconut trees.

Now, as we drove, Kit leaned against Paul's arm and fell asleep, breathing soundlessly against her father's pulse. All the way home, once you hit the Pali, is downward, a long sweep against softening hills, and at the bottom Paul stopped for ice cream, nudging Kit awake at the Chinese store.

"Shouldn't I just take you home first and then go unload the boat? Wouldn't it be a lot easier? I can take you home and double back."

For the second time during that ride I was disappointed. It was always strangely thrilling to visit Revere, to stand on the threshold of what might have been our house.

To avoid the traffic on Oneawa Street, or to satisfy that wish for something more exotic than the streets of our settled and respectable town offered, Paul took the swamp road over the last stretch of afternoon—a narrow, winding road through *halekoa* and *kiawe* trees. It is a place of birds and knee-high grasses— this ancient swamp — and on its high side, a huge landfill where bulldozers plow through the daylight hours, terracing the hillside with the rejected stuff — old beds and bureau drawers — of everybody's lives. Like ornamental carapaces, like the fossilized armor of prehistoric beasts, old metal skeletons of cars festoon the winding road below this burial ground.

Along the way, just visible behind a high wire fence, hangs what we called the Lady of the Swamp. Kit was the first to notice her one day soon after we arrived, aloft on her tree trunk. She stared past us unsmiling but not quite expressionless. Ship's maiden? Mannequin? Her wooden nakedness was so benevolent among the metal shards, her gesture was so eloquent, that we looked to her each time we drove by with expectation and anticipation.

Somewhere behind her the old *heiau* called Ulupo crumbles and dissolves. Its sacred stones lie scattered under silty water and marsh grass although part of its huge stone platform is still visible on a slight rise. A sign claims it was built by the *menehunes,* the earliest inhabitants, which means it has stood on that rise between the mountains and the sea for more than a thousand years. At that time we knew Mihana used to visit it every few days, walking around it, squinting up at it, trying to get a feel for its size and shape, tucking back into place—little by little—the fallen stones. She was a healer of some kind—the locals believed in her. But she was Christianized. All she had left of her heritage were stories and recipes for cures. People who had a need for cured stomachs or cured hearts still appeared sometimes at her door. Our door, Paul said.

Paul said Mihana shouldn't have inherited Revere. I think it seemed to him that she had locked him out of paradise and that because of it, no matter how polite she was, we were confined to a small rented house—in a Kailua tract built on old landfill.

The house, as we approached, looked small, but it was ours, where we lived with our mango tree, the flowering plumeria, the fig tree in the deep front yard, the growing be-still and the birds and small sounds of the place quietly humming. Paul turned the corner at a wide angle, driving slowly, being careful that the boat did not disturb the balance of our narrow and untraveled street; then let us out, telling me to take the bags and cooler, telling Kit to help me take the gear inside.

The cat wound himself around our feet, hungry and pleased to have us home. "Lukie...," Kit crooned. I ran a bath for Kit and urged her into it, then went outside the way I always did and walked around the mango tree. The shape and size of the old tree were comforting—almost what I remembered trees to be. Tall and tough and even-limbed, it looked almost deciduous, except that when they fell, the leaves were green. Beyond it, on the other side of the slat fence, a tall *kukui* tree seeded our yard daily with the hard black nuts the old Hawaiians used as lamps. They used to string them up on the spine of a banana leaf, then light the oil inside and count the hours as each *kukui* nut went out. Now they're made into necklaces and sold to tourists—there must be a million strings of them in Waikiki. I didn't mind about the seeds that lay in my yard. I took each tree at its face value. They didn't have to earn their keep or be domestic. I kept the garden trim but I let the trees be.

The one tree I took care of was the yellow be-still I had planted when we took the house. A seedling from Revere, I'd put it over the old cesspool right outside the living room, where, on its rich diet, it grew at an unnatural rate and bloomed continuously, its yellow flowers small bright torches that were always there. It was surrounded by the greens and reds and floral shapes and hues that grow so easily in gardens there. Without much effort things will bloom and multiply. And because the wall between the living room and the yellow tree was sliding glass and screen, the garden became part of the still, dark rooms where we lived. We became part of the garden.

From the garden, I looked inside and eyed the dented sofa and the mail. There was gear to unpack and a meal to get ready, but the old rattan sofa covered with pillows looked inviting. I could lie there and wait for Kit to finish her bath. I could stretch out and throw a magazine across my face or leaf through the envelopes of empty news, of bills and coupons that had piled up. I could lie there and think about Revere and what it was about it that had got into our skin, under our skin, buried head first like a chigger from my old Kansas backyard so that its tiny venom moved around in us, coursing as close as it could to our hearts.

I opened my back door, sliding it wide. After the winter rains, I knew the exact rumble of the wood and glass, the light resistance of the screen, so that I opened the door each time with a flourish as if, in that way, I could join the two worlds—outside and in. As if, having found a place to put down roots, I wanted to put them down in this ground on this island again and again.

There is no short season on the island. No brief summer moving into fall. The flowers bloom endlessly. Soon, I thought, we would belong here. The banana trees would feed us, and the mango trees and coconut palms.

I left the doors pushed back when I went in and peeled off shorts and shirt and underwear and went to the old sofa sleepily, reaching into the mail. The neighborhood was quiet at this hour. It was a Monday afternoon. The men were busy coming home. Soldiers and civil servants most of them. Women and children, back from jobs and school, waited for them. Except for us, this was a neighborhood of homeowners, of the middle class. Many were from the mainland—servicemen and businessmen and their wives. They shopped at Safeway for the most part although all the children went to the Chinese store close to the beach for shave-ice and crack seed. Children acclimatize. This was a neighborhood of childish dreams.

Paul would be pulling up the long, sandy driveway at Revere, trying to think of the best way to unload the heavy boat. He would have to cut across the grass at the only spot left unprotected by Mihana's hedge, then turn the whole thing around and back the car down to the beach. Or he would not drive as far as the house at all but use the boat ramp at the entrance to Lanikai, that thin strip of land hugging the cliffs. Revere covers ten acres of jungle and lawn at the far tip, inside the crotch of land where the ocean presses almost into it. The one-way road begins at the boat ramp, then circles Lanikai. The road, in its circle, passes through a different kind of neighborhood than ours. The houses on the beach had been built for the rich. Flower children lived in them now, and drug dealers and surfers, living communally. In the rest—in the smaller houses on the hill—there were families.

At the end of the road Mihana lived. Having no place more to go, the road turned around at Revere, and looped back out again.

Paul would use the boat ramp, I decided, and sail down to the old house, preferring the long walk back to the car when he was done. He would sail close to the shore because he had no light yet on the boat and he would think of the great, empty house ahead of him and of the times behind him when he had lived there, when he was a little boy. His disheveled childhood. Sent away to school at the age of nine, he had been an academic failure. He'd been looking toward Revere for years, wasting precious time. Now it was before him. He would see Maya running toward him in the darkness like a sandpiper, wild and thin and childishly excited, trying to stand still, trying to look poised, but forgetting and skipping around in that way she had because she was still a child. Inexperienced and untouched, Maya seemed closer to love and sex, and death than any of us. She was on the edge of it all, peering in. She had the hesitation of virginity. She would stare past us, into the windows, into the banyan tree, as if waiting for something, as if someone might arrive with an unimaginable message that would change everything. Or maybe it was something waiting for her behind the tree, ready to step out, and she was afraid but watching anyway so that she would recognize him when he came, dressed in colors of clay like the first man who had been created by the gods Lono and Kane on Makapuu Point, where the Marines lived.

Maya was wide-eyed, curious about everything, wandering in the jungle around Revere as if whatever was going to happen would happen there, as if knowing it would carry with it the strong smell of salt and blood.

Mihana kept her thoughts to herself. Perhaps everything was a danger, perhaps nothing. There were men everywhere. There were the Marines. There were the flower children with their drugs. They had come from California. They had come from far away. But Maya was too young to care, and Kailua had attractions for her; it sold the hibachis we took to the beach for week-end picnics, and throw-away diapers and rubber slippers and plastic jewelry and cigarettes. There were pizza places and a Korean restaurant and a small department store and a large drugstore. There were three streets which met the Pali highway. There was a gas station on every corner, and there was our house. Kailua was a town that might have been chipped out of the Midwest, except that in the center of it there was a patch of grass surmounted by a huge, clattering evening-full-of-birds banyan tree. Like the tree in Revere, only noisier, it functioned as the town clock, the scattering and regrouping of the mynah birds signaling morning and night. Kailua town—sleepy and self-satisfied, but vigilant, ready for some amusement, some entertainment, like Maya watching us.

I lay on our sofa, naked, knowing that by now the lights were on inside the small part of Revere that was inhabited, that Paul was relishing the thought of the cold beer he would drink there in the old house that looked, to him alone, in spite of termites and dry rot and a generation's softening decay, exactly as it had a quarter of a century before; that he was watching Maya running toward him, and Mihana standing on the slope above him, immense in front of the tall stand of ironwood that hid the house. And he would be glad he had come by water so as not to disturb the lawn, such as it was, or Mihana, such as she was. I lay on the sofa, our bills in hand, and thought about all that. I knew these things. I could follow Paul's course, I could look up the shore and through the dense jungle of ironwood trees that held the great and wasted lawn back from the collapsing beach. I could see where he passed and where he went—in which direction. Or so I thought. Just as I could listen to the song of Kit who would soon fall asleep in her bath and who would later blame me for it, although she lay in it like a snow angel, hair spread out around her head. She was making noises there now while the birds outside caroled and squawked their final evening messages, settling into trees, and while the neighbors in their matching small tract houses—mainlanders like us—settled around their dinners and TVs, and while the flowers opened their hearts and bodies suddenly and threw their fragrances into the air like offerings.

The cat, who sat outside on the well-clipped grass, listened along with me, and I held the unopened mail, believing there was no news that could matter very much to us anyway. Probably I should have felt just then a pull—a warning—that sense of small alarm that makes the hair rise on the neck's thin skin.

It was twilight, the hour when a mother calls her children home, and mine was here; my house was safe; my future still connected to my past. The press of Paul's hand, the color of Kit's hair, the things that I knew were all around. When the phone rang I got up to answer it as unprepared as I was unarmed.

THREE

"Sugar"—my mother's voice—"you better come home. He's back, Jesse. Your father," she added, in case I hadn't guessed.

There was the seashell whisper of long-distance cables between us, stretched across and under half the world. I could hardly hear her—that particular Midwestern voice. I was still thinking about Paul, Paul slowly drinking his beer. When I was three my father came home from the war and I locked myself in the bathroom of our house, and he had to carry a long extension ladder around to the upstairs window and climb up and pry me out of the place. We descended together. He carried me on his back; he held my beanstalk wrists inside one hand. The neighbors were lined up on the sidewalk watching. He was finally home again.

Paul found me in the ugly water Kit had left cold in the tub, knees poking up through its grayness, arms floating, all these extremities like drowning creatures half submerged.

"We have to leave," I said vacantly, having made reservations for the three of us. And I explained.

He brought me a glass of red wine and said he'd start the packing. Had I eaten yet?

He found Kit in her room where I had led her from the bath, in a sleeping crumple of clothes and sheets and towels, where I had patted her hair into damp peaks and rubbed the towel over and down the smooth, sleepy surface of her body and leaned her into the flowered bedding, past the toys and animals, stepping around the doll house and its scattered furniture, the Checkers and Pogo record player and the Barbie dolls. Past and around all that, into the flowered hold. Then I had put myself into her gray bath.

In the bathroom mirror Paul studied his face which did not have complicated features or expressions. He was thirty-four years old but he still wore the blond, disingenuous look of a boy. Turning the faucet on and wetting first his hands and then his hair he turned around to look at me, as if he didn't understand. "Where was he then? All those years?"

When I met him, Paul was as bland as a peeled egg. Not a hair on his chest, either—no sign of the man to be. Paul and I met when I was still a child eighteen years old and we saved everything excessive for the years ahead. We met each other unrevealed and grew together like saplings, side by side, like sibling trees, using the same air and light and soil until we came to look and feel almost alike.

Drying his face, Paul mumbled into the towel, "I'll get the suitcase down." Going out he left the door open so that the room began to cool and drops of moisture appeared on the surface of the mirror and ran slowly toward the corners. I heard him rummaging in the kitchen and in the hall closet and in the laundry room, finding enough clean clothes to organize. He even did a load of wash and I sat on in the cold water, watching the palms of my hands wrinkle up as if they were old.

At last I climbed out to find him folding and packing Kit's clothes, lingering as fondly over each shirt and each pair of shorts as he would over a memory, showing me by his precision that he had no choice.

"I can't go with you, honey," he said. "I have to be here for the show at that gallery. You know how much it means. This guy has a magazine too. I could turn the corner on this one, Jess, and get out of commercial stuff." Paul was as faithful to his vocation as he was to me. He was fingering dresses. His blue eyes regarded me. What I loved about him was his utter sincerity. "But I hate this. I hate to have you go alone."

I watched in silence as he ate a peanut-butter sandwich, and when he had finished packing we went to bed covered in shyness. The birds had long before settled; the night sounds of the garden were completely stilled. The hibiscus flowers were folded up. Even the background thumps of the old kitchen fridge, heart of the house, had stopped. Goodbyes as unfamiliar to us as death, we were embarrassed by a mutual defection—and lay next to each other carefully apart.

Our farewells the next day weren't much good. I wasn't used to traveling alone. I'd only gone home alone once, pregnant with Kit, claimed by my husband's surreptitious seed and freed of my father's absent authority. Paul had claimed me, that was the way I looked at it; I was his, and through each other we were identified. And now at the airport, his face, like blotting paper, had an uneven color as he held onto our bags until there was nothing left to do but guide us through the assorted tour groups going back to the mainland in bright aloha shirts.

Paul took us to a dreary bar over the runway. I remember its dark colors and the three of us huddled in a brown corner taking a last look at each other. A troop plane with thumbnail windows was visible through the wall of smoked glass, bound for southeast Asia, for Vietnam, and we watched it hopelessly, as if I'd been called to service, drafted by my father's reappearance, and the outcome of our separation would be tragedy. Perhaps in spite of our politics, our pacifism, we felt ashamed or left out because somewhere, without us, the war of our generation was still going on.

Paul ordered an uncharacteristic glass of Scotch and took a Valium out of the packet he kept folded in his wallet. He held it carefully between his thumb and forefinger until the drinks arrived, as if determined to exhibit pain, even in this small, thin-coated form, in the face of my adventure. Already numb, whatever I had to drink made me more stupid and frightened and detached, but Paul held the sliver of Valium aloft like a small, white communion wafer—this is my body—because he wasn't going to Kansas and he wasn't going out on the troop plane.

"Remember Daddy loves you, honey," he said, stroking Kit's hair, brushing it against his sleeve, sipping his drink. He was wearing his blue shirt, his cowboy boots, his jeans. "Make me some pictures of the goldfish, sweetheart. I packed your pens. And don't forget your old dad."

"Mom let me go to sleep in the bathtub." Her dress damp where his face had leaned against it, Kit crumpled against him, too big for his lap, unwilling to give him up to come away with me. We left a large tip and stumbled out into the afternoon, into the racket and commotion of the airport where tourists were taking their final snapshots and those on tours were getting the requisite tour-group orchid lei. It was a long walk to the gate. But Paul stayed with us all the way.

On the plane, with Kit beside me, I slept and flew for hours that were unmarked, from tropic to Midwest in one long nap. I leaned against the window with my eyes closed thinking of childhood, and a woman across the aisle played Old Maid with Kit. Next to me, by the window, a huge Samoan held his head in his hands. All through the flight he groaned as if in pain. He was wearing a starched white shirt and thick polished shoes but—as if caught between worlds—he was tightly wrapped from his waist to his socks in a dark cloth in the Polynesian way.

"We have birds called egrets that eat bugs off the cows in the swamp," Kit confided to the card player, pushing a button and leaning back importantly. "At school we get leis on our birthday and we don't have to wear shoes. You know what leis are, don't you? Like that lady has on. Flowers on string. I made one. Didn't you get one for the plane?" Ours were in a plastic bag in the compartment overhead. I wanted to save one for my mother, and one for my father too. Kit rattled on. "Only school's out right now. I only went to school last year. My dad went there too, when he was little, before he moved away. Even my grandmother did. My teacher is Mrs. Oshiro. No! Was. Last year, I mean." Kit chortled and snapped her tray table up and down. She bounced in her seat. "And now my grandfather came back." The Samoan moaned. "My dad's a photographer. What color do you like the best? Black has them all in it. Did you know that? We got a new boat. That's why I like red the best."

The woman was delighted. She dealt the cards. Kit said, "We wear long dresses called muumuus. You prob'ly saw them, didn't you?"

They discussed life in the islands while I pretended to sleep, dreaming that the space between two places, between past and present, could be reduced to a few hours with a book, a pillow, and a deck of cards.

I woke to the basket weave of the landscape below as we began our slow descent, hanging over the Kansas River, the brown, complacent Kaw, over the fields set out and plowed along ideal and rigid lines of property, over small creeks and hedgerows and fences. The river here swings across a valley. It swings in an ever-widening arc until a run of fast water or a flood cuts down into another layer of the land. Then, for a while, the river straightens up, leaving the towns along its curves high and dry for years before it returns, cutting across the valley again like a meandering snake. We hung above the mud-colored, winding river that wet-nursed green and yellow wheat and alfalfa and soybeans and corn. We descended into the landscape and it was like coming into old age unprotesting, where everything loomed large. We floated into it, angling down in the strict, yellow haze, the flat light of the Midwest, and then settling onto the stark line of ground.

At the airport in Kansas City, everyone was the same color. Everyone was cut from the same mold. We have inherited the earth, I thought, suddenly surprised. We come from nowhere. We belong nowhere. As a race we are young. We take what we want and move on.

My mother's sisters had been sent to meet us and I threw myself at both of them, noticing their changes as they noticed mine. They said the usual things about Kit—her hair, her height, her eyes, her skin—the picture of my mother at that age—placing her between them in the front seat and me in the back seat with my purse.

"So the Chevy's still running," I drawled, finding my home voice, sinking into the back seat of this car I'd known them to arrive in on countless Sunday afternoons—two maiden aunts who lived in the same town, same five-bedroom hotel, where they'd been born. The car's cool interior had seemed to match their temperaments. Because of my mother's solitary state, they often stayed with us for days. For days we would be a household of women, my mother, my aunts, my grandmother when she was still alive, and me.

"Afraid you're too late." The aunt speaking didn't turn her head. "Or did your mother tell you already?" They handed back a thermos full of coffee and a shoe box full of cookies as if I were a child to be appeased. Then they told me with sighs of evident satisfaction that my father had indeed come home. "But sometime during the night he passed on." They said it as if this was their last chance in our shared lives to point out that he had fulfilled every expectation they might have had.

"Died with his boots on, too," one of them put in.

"His suitcase was still packed." They didn't share my mother's romantic view of family life.

"How is it out there, dear? How is it out there? In Hawaii? Tell us about it all anyway...."

But I said nothing. They had tricked me. My mother had tricked me into coming home, looking for him. My father had lived so long in my imagination, it was impossible, without my willing it, for him to die.

In the front seat, Kit bolted up and began to speak, moistening her lips first and clearing her throat: "We wear long dresses and we——" But I couldn't rely on her description for these two. Better that the place I'd landed sound as ordinary as I could make it sound. Why tempt the local gods. "It's nice," I said. "Safeways and running water and highways and all."

"At least he died in the right bed," the one who was driving said.

I bit my tongue and focused on the scenery, remembering why I never visited. We have to keep the truths we know safe from conflicting points of view. I'd worked for years against these two to keep my own beliefs intact.

"At least your poor mother has her dignity."

"When you took off, we never saw a thing of you after that," said the one, who seemed to be squeezing Kit under her wing. "Now it's Hawaii. First it was Colorado and Arizona and California and where all."

You've come back at last, she meant to say, but not for us. And where's your father? Disappointing you as usual. And *he's* the one you come to see....

For miles and miles, like a magnet pulling us across its surface, the turnpike rose and dipped and straightened while we made Christian conversation and my two aunts concealed, to some extent, the pleasure they took in this occasion. Relishing the scene of reunion and death, carrying me back, by force, to childhood.

"Here's Kilmer. What's left of it."

A railroad signal, long defunct, some tracks, a few scattered houses and family bones.

FOUR

The house was all shade and high ceilings—the center of my Kansas childhood. A deep porch wrapped two sides. Once it had seemed enormous to me, when I was very young, then it had been merely sufficient, growing smaller, cramped and stifling, as I grew out of it. As we drove up the little street where I had lived for eighteen years, the house changed again in perspective. It grew on us as we approached and then seemed to shrink again, to slump into its surroundings like an already tired host, and by the time we pulled into the driveway it was a small box, a thing of the past, with my relatives pressed against the glass of the windows and squeezed against the door.

Remembered, familiar, its home smell rushed up at me like flesh the minute I opened the back door and pushed Kit into the kitchen.

All those blue eyes! And faces that looked enough like mine to assume kinship. Most of them I hadn't seen since early childhood but there was that tendency to long bones and large features that marks each one of us. Reflected faces all around the kitchen table, at the stove and at the tiled counter, as if trick mirrors had been installed. Even the dark circles under our eyes are uniform. (Stopping for gas at a service station when I was a child, my mother was told by the man pumping gas that the circles under my eyes were sure signs of a heart condition. After that, she assumed I wasn't long for this world.) An incessant dreaming in the men, supportive dreams among the women. We seem to marry our own kind. What I saw in our faces was a downward tendency. When I walked in, everyone formal and solemn, I held each of them in turn, hungry for their bones and hair and skin. The family touch. Hungry for my own.

My father was missing. Nothing had changed. He had escaped us all again and, strangely, the unlikely gathering was being held for him.

I was pulled from the grasp of cousins left standing at the kitchen table. The aunts were supervising. They had us in tow. Kit and I were guided through the darkened house, where shades were pulled and where the carpeting and walls reeked of this last betrayal by my father. Where even the chairs and lamps disapproved of his late arrival, my late arrival. And where I could hear the family behind us murmuring as we tiptoed up the creaking stairs.

Taking Kit's hand, I led her to the foot of my mother's bed, which was covered with the same spread, the same faded sheets, the same afghan I could remember from visits to the room during the nightmares that had plagued my childhood. There were the same flowers on the spread and the same grapes and pears. But they were all a shade lighter now, as if they'd been worn away by the faith of my mother, as if they'd been made threadbare by her unloved body as she lay waiting for him—and maybe even for me, after I left so many years ago.

Faded, too, my mother, who sat precariously on the edge of the bed as if she could not allow herself a day of rest or as if my father's fresh absence, the untouched pillowcase behind her, made it impossible for her to lie down there at all.

Kit's seven years seemed unequal to the pale grandmother, tipped now against the wooden headboard, staring down drowsily. She pulled away.

"She didn't sleep much on the plane," I offered lamely, kissing my mother's cheek. Kit knocked one shoe against the other. She was unaccustomed to hard soles after her barefoot year and, after all her talk on the plane and in the car, she looked bored and blank.

"Don't mind," my mother said, dabbing at the air between us as if to clear it. She leaned forward, scowling a little in her effort to focus on Kit. "She seems to be her father's daughter," she said vaguely, licking her lips. Perhaps she had doubted this. "Where is my kiss?" She bowed her head. Then she simply looked up, as if considering the next order of business, and licked her lips again, which were dry and as colorless as if her own blood had been lost in this death.

She said, "Kit, I believe, has the back bedroom." Her eyes looked bruised. She moved a hand. "You have your own."

Kit looked up, relieved, seeing me become child, as I stood there apologetic and uncomforting, awkward and already sullen, looking away.

"I'll take you down to see him when you've hung up your wrinkled clothes," Mother said, taking charge at last. "I always told you he'd come back, didn't I, Jess." Tomorrow she would tell me how to iron the wrinkled clothes, how to sprinkle them and wrap them in a tea towel and put them in the fridge for an hour first.

"Those are your cousins on your father's side," she said as if she'd accomplished a social feat in bringing them here. "Be nice to them." We had strict rules of hospitality.

It was a Kansas June, when courtrooms used to forgo business and close up. Once there had been no lawsuits, no divorces, no reprisals in the summer heat. My mother used to stand outside the house in the hot sun, hoping my father wouldn't notice her as she leaned there listening, ear to the window frame, waiting for him to play his piano again. But he would never play when she was anywhere near. She had heard him play in the hotel once when

35

they were introduced, after which, no matter how often she asked him for a song, he had refused. Whenever I looked at the outside of the house now, it almost seemed some faint impression of my mother's younger self was still visible there. In this house there were dreams in the closets and under the floorboards and inside the walls. Sometimes they clung to the windowpanes so that we could almost have touched them; sometimes they obscured our view. We were aware of them in the drafts of air that we could see stirring the drapes.

"You believe for one minute that he would not be here for Christmas? Your father is a sentimental man. You think anything at all would keep him from us but extreme necessity?" my mother used to ask me, searching my look, my posture, even my hands for some trace of disbelief.

I'd nod. On Christmas Eve I always read the story of the prodigal son in my white plastic Bible, sitting in bed, dressed in my flannel nightgown. I kept the place marked with a ribbon and a palm-leaf cross. It was the only thing I read before I turned out the light.

My mother grew up in the hotel in Council Grove near railroad tracks put there so her grandfather could drive huge locomotives across the countryside. It seemed to her that the Atchison, Topeka and Santa Fe tracks and the Union Pacific tracks were the arms of the continent. When she met my father, she must have smelled on him the curiously perfumed essence of a moving train.

My father's brief and ardent life. Being his daughter. Being of one substance with him. Who might have taken me away. Who might have carried me into unknown regions. Who offered me as sacrifice and disappeared.

And my mother ordered the Sunday *New York Times* which arrived on Tuesdays and she filed its many articles under convenient headings in shoe boxes, for shoes were her passion, so her two consuming and civilizing passions were perfectly met — of her feet and of her mind—perfectly fit. She kept up with the probable destinations of my father and she kept fashionably shod. He's an ankle man, she said.

My mother bore me as a hedge against the war, in case my father should disappear into it, just as I used Kit now against the war, to keep Paul from disappearing into it. As long as he was a father and a married man, he was exempt. The pink paper announcing my pregnancy to the draft board saved him from Vietnam. We were afraid of it, the war in Vietnam, a terrible turnpike down which everybody sped. Families are invented around war, or vice versa. You're a war baby, my mother always said. You're my exemption, Paul had said, as if babies and war fit together, inspired each other.

After my clothes were dutifully hung up, my mother met me downstairs and drove me to the funeral parlor on Mission Street. My father lay in a room full of flowers. My mother led me to the door, as if to introduce me to the one who had been larger than life to me for as long as I could remember. His tiny scrawl on postcards, week after week for years, my own mythology. Pike's Peak. I made it, love, your Dad. On the road to Shanghai. Halfway there, love, your Dad. A great place. Love Dad. Wish you were here. Dad. Each card, smaller than life but all I had, was treasured by both of us. But Mother took my arm and drew me to the suffocation of that room, and then she left me there alone with him. Left us alone and I stood at the door; I pressed against it, exhaling and forgetting to breathe in again.

He lay, condemned, away from me. How could he be reduced to this? How could he be reduced to flesh, this dancer, covered from the waist down in the stiff lap robe of casket as if he'd accepted a magician's challenge and been sawn in half?

Outside a crow screamed. Inside nothing stirred. I was alone and not alone. His helplessness left me no cover. I was not prepared to give up his spirit which had been with me, in one form or another, before I was able, even, to recognize it. I wanted some gesture that would recreate him now that I had him finally at hand.

"Father," I muttered, superstitiously. "Daddy," afraid now of his silence more than I ever had been of his voice, his reality.

I took a step. I crept a little closer and carefully looked down.

The suit he had arrived in.
A mustache I didn't know he had.
Large hands.
A borrowed tie.
A wedding ring.
I couldn't think of anything that I'd want him to suffer for.

We buried my father as close as we could to the house. As if it mattered any more. There were hymns played on a portable electric organ and we sat on folding metal chairs around a raw hole in the ground protected from the sun by a piece of canvas stretched on outward-leaning poles. The coffin was suspended somehow under it. It seemed that if we stood up and abandoned our positions, it would disappear for ever, taking my father with it into dark ground.

Uncertainly we sang, "Come to the church in the wild wood, oh come to the church in the vale. No spot is so dear to my childhood as the little brown church in the vale...." Except for our small party, the cemetery was still, stretching away for acres on all sides of us. Hats in hands, everyone seemed to wait. He'd been so briefly with us, it seemed we might, perhaps, stay for a while.

What I want is a sacrament, I thought. I want a rite. For the same reason I had Kit baptized—the water, oil, and salt were bound to have some primitive effect, to leave a mark. My mother stood up and sighed. Inside her white suit, behind her dark glasses, she appeared to tremble for a moment, while the old, dry lakebed prepared itself for my father's bones. She was no longer abandoned. He was no longer missing. He had come back to her. He was at her feet now, a decorated soldier. She held out her hands for the flag which was folded carefully into sections and handed across into her keeping.

We should have trimmed his nails and hair, I thought, taking her arm. And kept them, buried, underneath the house.

FIVE

The days following were hot, and the nights brought no relief. I hadn't heard from Paul. Rootless, I walked the bare wood of the halls in my bare feet knocking at doors. My bed, my childhood bed, became a yawning, sweaty hole and I avoided it. I wandered from one talking face to another, from one bedroom to another, getting to know the aunts, the recent histories of friends, and variations on my life the family found acceptable.

Like my childhood mattress, which held the imprint of my shape like grass that has been slept on by an animal, the Kansas house was full of vacant and regretful impressions of my father's cumulative time there, which amounted to not much more than five years all told. There was a picture of him by a wooden lawn chair in the back yard in his Navy uniform. There was a wall of postcards and snapshots in my mother's room that she had kept up sporadically, over the years. A picture of his parents' shiny black De Soto, the only new car they ever had, my father standing next to it in store-bought shirt and pants. Pinned to the wall there were mementoes like three ticket stubs to a Chautauqua he'd attended, and his train ticket to Council Grove.

I wandered in the forgotten heat of childhood, when it was so oppressive we threw ice water on our sheets before we went to bed. The heat could be a thickness in the room. Now I could feel my father with us in the house, checking on the potential wheeze, the undigested meat. Noticing dripping faucets, unpaid bills. Unwilling to relinquish his last hold on us.

Under the open windows of a bedroom where I'd waited for him every night for years, I lay awake. Returning after midnight, he'd shut the lights off one by one, check all the doors, and climb the stairs. As familiar as my own heartbeat, that sound of creaking stairs, moving toward me through the dark.

Often on these hot nights I wondered why I couldn't hold my mother in the dark and stroke her hair and let her face cry on my arm. But I could not. The only refuge in the whole thick house was in Kit's bed and I crept in there every night, adjusting to her little back as Paul had curled to mine now for twelve years.

"Tell me about the lakes," she'd whisper ardently, as if the past that spoke here was a distant, foreign one the whisper of which I'd already heard. As if I could decipher it.

"They drained them off when everyone got poor," I'd tell her, sniffing at her hair which smelled like bread dough rising in the sun. "They left the house like this, beached on this little rise, surrounded by Great-grandpa's dried-up sea...."

I told her about my mother and father too. Family romance, I told her. They met in 1939 and fell in love like pure geometry. He wrote for newspapers—small articles about small towns. After the war he brought a bracelet home for me—a gold bracelet a dying sailor gave him for me....

But soon Kit was asleep. And all around us the old evidence of wet. Toes scratched in dirt uncovered generations of fish bones. My family's water love. Lakes gone before I came, long disappeared, dissolved, and vanished into mud for farmland. Earth reclaimed. The street we lived on known as Lakeside but dry as a whistle, my grandmother used to say.

During the mornings I stayed home with Mother, packing things. My father's clothes, mute and impotent relics now, were cast away. She knew they contained nothing she could rely on.

His medals from the war, his letters to her then, even his watch and personal effects were given to the Salvation Army. Like the insignia of a private cargo cult, they'd served their purpose; they had brought him back.

"You kept that stuff for years." My mother had worked in a library. She had it cataloged and arranged in drawers.

"But not any more. I don't need it all now. I have him here."

My mother used to tell people that he was traveling for his work. This went on for years. Hearing her, I'd imagine vast seas and highways, great ships and trains on which he traveled in disguise. I had no idea why he did this. I had no idea what went on between a husband and a wife. When he was home after the war I'd watched them from the distance of my room or, better, from the safety of the yard. Even my mother became a stranger to me. Afterwards I would remember us as families are supposed to be. I saw us at a table or my mother in the kitchen or my father working on a project—fixing the lawnmower was a favorite. I saw us the way I wanted us—a perfect triangular unity.

Now I found my way into the hot, oven-like attic, away from everyone, where Mother had stored away my scrapbooks, letters, yearbooks, programs, diaries, and drawings. She must have felt reminders of my past were less distracting than the relics left by Father. Perhaps she expected me to appear seasonally like the Hawaiian gods, to renew her supply. I came across a box of letters Paul had written. "Darling," he had scribbled, "we will never have a bread-and-peanut-butter life." Courting through the mails that first childish summer while he drove around in his old truck, taking pictures, doing things like tractor ads and farm loan ads, I was "the whisper in his ear". I was eighteen. I was a virgin; I had saved myself for him. Suddenly I missed him. I thought about his hands, and then his eyelids which were dusty violet, and his peeling sunburned flesh; his body was like his character, tender one moment and withdrawn the next. When we ran off together we were moving from one place to another, from town to town, taking pictures to sell to magazines, and having Kit. I left the letters where they were, but took a box of towels and kitchen things that had been given to us after we eloped, so long ago, and never used.

Did Father play the piano for Mother in the end, I wondered fitfully. But I never asked. It was part of our deep alliance, part of the loyalty to my mother that was buried in the painful past when we had lived together, abandoned as if we'd sinned. Being together reminded us again that we were not sufficient without him.

During the afternoons I'd take Kit for long rides, the way my mother used to take me out in the car. In Kansas people did this on a Sunday afternoon, or on a summer evening. Midwestern summer—the texture of its browns and greens, the flash of scarlet against mud in the color of a bird or wildflower, cool shade trees over hot ground. Here Paul had courted me. I lay against his thighs, between his thighs, my clothes open and adrift around us on the tall grass so the smell of him, mixed with the fields, stayed with me, and he placed his hands behind me, pressing my body to his face. I had forgotten—how could I?—that wave of grass, the prairie rolling on, the squirrel rush and the flattened sleeping place of deer, the farm sounds on side roads ignored by everyone but us. I had forgotten. I had moved away carrying lightweight baggage and a light heart.

Nothing was left of old Captain Kilmer's place, the house after which our small town was named. When I was growing up, the house was over there, stained and cracked, across a road and field north of ours. It was the oldest place in the vicinity and it had been kept up to some extent. It must have been too grand for the surrounding countryside, inspiring envy so that pieces of it were carried away, its stones and window frames and doors removed to other house sites, carried off in wagons and on backs after his death, his property picked clean. In other fields there were stone walls, dry walls like old Hawaiian ones but stouter, of gray stone. Because there were no trees the ancestors used this stone for everything. Cleared from the fields, stone grew into barns first, then houses—the earliest ones were made of sod. Stone walls enclosed animals, then graves. Mile after mile, we passed empty stone houses, huge hollow barns, and gravestones where the inscriptions had been lost.

Sometimes Kit and I played in those old wrecks of houses, making tables, pretending to bake bread, pretending bread and meat were eaten there. Everything about that pioneer family life seemed ideal to us. We imagined ideal ancestors.

In early evening I'd catch lightning bugs and rub them on my arms and Kit's so that we'd glow. We'd listen for the screaming pulse of crickets—the metronome of a summer night. Nights when the crickets didn't scream meant something dangerous was in the air.

At home my mother wandered in her back yard checking on rosebushes and fish, a sister on each arm. They were finally pleased with life, with its retributions, and they were even pleased enough with me. I had a husband who was, if nothing else, loyal to me.

My aunts finally packed up their clothes and sisterly good deeds and went away. I had an urge to do the same. We had not heard a word from Paul. I thought of calling him, but I didn't. I sent him a telegram instead, telling him my father was dead.

In Kansas you can feel the weather come. And you can hear it in the insects. Warned by the crickets, we would rush outside at signs of a tornado and take off in a car to find a hill to watch the great mile-high tunnel black as the inside of space rushing toward us as if we'd called it over the purple field. In Kansas even the summer storms appearing out of nowhere drop over you like blankets of the night. They fall on you, and you become invisible, and you drive through them wondering if you're blind.

Out in the back yard, Mother walked with us—granddaughter trailing behind carrying a box of oatmeal for the goldfish. Mother was looking at the brook my father built. He built a pump for it and a waterfall. He lined it with flagstones. One winter after he left all the fish froze in the ice. She chopped them out and they lay perfect in the snow, great golden fan tails shimmering as if she had the power of resurrecting life.

At our feet her goldfish fanned their broad tails and waited. "Have you made up your minds to settle down?" I knew what was coming—we had the same conversation whenever she phoned—and I cringed. "A man of his age," she said slowly. "What is he now? Thirty-five?"

"Four."

"Well, that's what I mean, sugar. You're still getting that allowance or whatever you call it?"

"Yes. From the estate." This subject always embarrassed me.

"Still. You're luckier than me at least. You're a real family. Like this," Mother said to Kit, sprinkling oatmeal over the fish to rouse their appetites and bring them close. Ticking away at my life, which was predictable, she said, she answered any questions she ever raised.

"Does he still have to stay away from that place to get the money?"

I pushed my hair back. "You mean Revere." It was a hot afternoon and I, to please my mother, was wearing a dress and underwear. Kit fed the fish happily. She was blossoming. She actually grew taller in the demanding air. As family members faded into the highways, Mother attached herself to Kit. They went to my mother's hairdresser, where Kit's hair was cut. My mother was a great one for appearances. Sit up straight, she'd say a hundred times a day. Let's have no hair in those blue eyes. They went to the Museum of Indian Remains and an art exhibit at a nearby shopping mall. I stayed behind. I idled in my mother's house. I was reluctant to go out, avoiding people who might claim to be old friends. A few of them stopped by with the quick appraising stares of people left behind, offering casseroles. I was ashamed of my fortune as if I had escaped. They lived correctly. They had jobs and law offices. They had car agencies. They were good husbands and wives. But I thought I would not have lasted long among them. I thought I was only fit for my peculiar life.

My mother knew that I was eager to be off. She smelled it in my skin. She saw it in my look. I saw the airplane as deliverance. No ghosts could follow me aboard and I would be delivered, with my boarding pass, into the present, which was where I thought we lived. I called out the names of our Hawaiian streets, hearing their sounds, conjuring them subtly, like serpents, like erotic beauties with foreign names, locating them in my mind: Beretania Street. Fort Street. King Street. Kalakaua Street. Queen Street. Those royal streets. I only knew a few names of the kings. But there was Princess Kaiulani, young and beautiful, who had a garden full of peacocks, who knew Robert Louis Stevenson, who would have been queen, who died at the age of twenty-three. All of them died tragically.

"And what about you, sugar?" Speaking to Kit. "What's in your cards?"

"Don't worry, I'm gonna be famous, Gramma. Just wait and see." Kit spun around, flinging out her arms and knocking a plastic lawn chair to its knees.

Putting the box down, Mother frowned. "Famous for what?"

Kit didn't know. "For dancing," she tried casually. "I'm gonna be a dancer and I'll sing too prob'ly, if I want."

We resumed our old places at the table, Mother and I, only now we had Kit between us, Kit and I remembering to sit up straight, to handle our knives and forks properly for my mother's sake. Each night we ate another casserole.

"Were you ever famous, Gramma?"

My mother hesitates.

"Was Granny Tilson then? The one who had the gun. Mom's grandmother. You know. That one?"

"What?"

47

"Was she a pioneer?"

"Granny Tilson? No, not quite...."

"Mom says she almost had to shoot a man." Loving the image, Kit sights down her arm straight at the glass my mother holds, sees Alice at the window listening, hearing the man approaching outside on the path, out by the water pump, outside the house, boots crunching bold because he knew she was alone.

"Kit honey, don't point," my mother says. "He'd paid your great-grandmother some money that day. That's right. Yes."

Kit says, "It was a Saturday and he came back because the banks were closed. Weren't they? He knew the money was still there in the house. Then she yelled at him." Kit tilts her head and booms out, " 'I've got a gun up here at this window! Don't you take one more step. I'm going to sit right here with this gun all night.' "

"Kit. I said let's don't point, dear. It's rude. It's violent."

While in the cradle at her side my father lay, absorbing the event. And my tough-minded grandmother would tell the story on the smallest pretext.

"She heard him in the dark," Kit says, already knowing all the lines.

"She knew he was there," I say.

"That's right."

When Mother drove us to the airport we had been gone three weeks. Kit was quiet in the back seat. With all the windows up and the air conditioner going full blast, we rolled across the prairie again, the air so hot and full that the wheat fields wavered through the glass.

"Gramma," Kit said, "I want the window down. Okay?"

"No, Kit. It makes us too hot. And the wind's too strong."

Kit waited a bare minute. Then she said, "Gramma. I need to."

My mother's fingernail, painted an unlikely red, pushed the button at her side and down the window rolled. Saying nothing, glancing around at me and back at Kit, she added up regrets. Under her gaze, I slouched beside my closed glass, looking out at the scenery.

I used to imitate my mother—the way she used clothes and jewelry and perfume to become more than my mother. But Kit, her window down, leaned out into the air and put her head back unselfconsciously as if the wind, roaring into the tunnel of her throat, would ease her way to stardom. Then she began to sing.

SIX

At the other end of the day, where Paul waited, it was late afternoon. The sun behind our plane made the shadow on the water below look like a small, black island floating just ahead of us. The islands were there in fact, each of them mentioned in the captain's airline drawl as we flew over them. "...This one's called the Big Island, folks. What you see over there in the distance is the volcanoes, Mauna Koa and Kilauea, home of the fire goddess Pele, who still sends up plenty of fire. If you're planning any visits up there to her residence, you'd be well advised to take an offering. I hear she's real fond of gin. Next below now of course is Maui, second largest in the chain, formed by two volcanoes which are asleep. At least we hope. The island off the point is Kahoolawe, and we'll have Molokai on our left in a minute now. It was joined to Maui before the ocean rose. On its north side is still a settlement for people suffering from leprosy or Hansen's Disease, who are perfectly free these days to come and go, although that wasn't always the case. In the distance—Lanai. Owned by the Dole Company. They grow your sliced pineapple over there. Well now. Looks like good weather down there, folks. We're approaching the island of Oahu, home of most of the islands' population. The windward side is visible around the eastern bend just ahead. Although folks out here don't tend to use directionals like that. They talk a different language—mauka—toward the mountains—and makai, the sea. You better get used to it or you'll get lost. Mauka now, as we turn, there's another defunct crater, well known as Diamond Head. Under her, you have Waikiki. This world-famous resort was once the sporting place of chiefs. Now there's the Royal Hotel, the Pink Lady she was called in her day. Thank you for flying with us, folks. Aloha. Now kindly remain in your seats...."

But I stood up while we taxied down the runway, unable to wait, suddenly aware of myself as the returning wife and feeling missed; aware of Paul as someone who would be real again in moments, there to be touched again, there to absorb my point of view. I was reassured, as I'd been for years, at the notion of myself as Paul's wife.

In the terminal, Paul stood alone, away from the stampede of tourists, as if he had forgotten who he was looking for, or why he had come. He was wearing his cowboy boots, work-shirt, and jeans — even his silver-buckled belt, from which, when he saw us, he unhooked his thumbs. A mix of excitement and shyness came over me. In spite of the familiar clothes, he seemed different. But Kit ran to him. We'd stepped into all the familiar foreignness of Honolulu. Everything felt unreal.

"Your bags are miles away," Paul said, taking Kit with him through the crowd, sure, now, why he had come. He eyed me once or twice and I thought, well, he's greedy for me too.

"You never even got to see him, did you? After all that."

"At least now I know what he looked like.... For years I thought he was a trick of my memory."

Once we were out of the arrival area, the soft air met us like a bath—something we could taste and feel and smell—and I drank in the landscape, thirsty from the long, dry light of Kansas. All the way home I was tasting it and touching it and sniffing at the flower scent that went before us and came after us—in fact encircled us because we were encumbered by Paul's leis. To be given flowers at the airport is to become part of the island, to be veiled in a new identity. You want to take off your stockings and mainland shoes. You want to let your hair down and lean back and relax and let the trade wind, with its smells and promises, blow right over you. I looked around, wanting to nourish myself on the instant, the great relief of homecoming, but feeling strangely out of place, feeling, in spite of myself, divided. I looked at the highway construction and trucks. I looked at the starchy bougainvillea and the flowering trees. The world outside our car sucked at my skin. Sounds of the traffic, sounds of a barking dog, a screaming newsboy in the center of the road, jack-hammers, birds, the overpowering, sweet stench of cooking pineapple at the Dole factory, and, behind, the salty, blood-thick smell of the sea.

Paul's hands were on the steering wheel and he looked out at everything as if he belonged to it. His back was straighter. His expression was relaxed, assured. After a change you notice things. You see things differently. You notice what you've missed before or left undone.

"Kelly's Drive-In," he announced with a sweep of his window arm. "Home of da kind best stew and taro bread. You want? Kit? Want me go stop?" He was putting on his local accent, speaking in pidgin. "Just say the word. You want to know the truth, there's not too much to eat at home."

I didn't want to stop. I wanted to drive up the highway with new eyes, seeing this place the way Paul saw it, seeing this island the way Paul wanted it to be. Old missionary houses, white and straight-edged, lined our way. Families who had been here for generations, who were halfway between the Hawaiians and me.

"Three weeks," said Paul. "And probably forgot how to swim already, for sure, didn't you?"

"No, not," said Kit in the local way. Children in the islands have a kind of shorthand pidgin of their own and now Kit was assuming it—throwing it around because she felt at home. "How's Lukie boy? My bad cat."

"He caught a lizard every single day. I swear. I saved them for you. They're on your bed."

"I better have a little talk with Luke," Kit chirped. "Hey! Did you get me my new skates yet?"

"How was the show?" I said. There was a truck spoiling the view ahead, full of bouncing trash.

"There's a closing party tomorrow night. We're having dinner at Revere first." Paul lifted his shoulders as if they hurt.

A tiny, cone-shaped peak, piece of the mountainside, stood out on our left. Covered entirely by the soft hair of pine, it was a chip of the razor-thin Koolaus, the mountain range that cuts the island into halves, the barrier that wrapped around us and blocked everything ahead as we went up and up toward the double tunnels in a wall of lava rock.

"Okay. This time anyone want to see the site of the victory?" Paul pulled off and drove up a winding road. I didn't like the lookout. I said, "Kit's in a hurry to get home."

The Pali is a place of power and winds, its cliff so abrupt and terrible they say the island chain was finally conquered and united when Kamehameha applied himself to it, driving the opposing forces of Oahu up Nuuanu Valley ahead of him and then sending them over the edge into the fierce, windward abyss. But it wasn't like that really. Mihana is descended from those Oahu chiefs and she knows the truth, or so she says. Only a few went over, and they died a noble death. They jumped rather than be taken captive.

Here ancient gods hurl warnings. The wind blows against you so hard you have to hang on to the rail. We stood between separate worlds. We saw before us a great bowl, with the sky across from us as the far edge and, below, layers of every shade of green: the deep green of moist pastures of sugar cane, the yellow green of thick banana trees, the blue green of the Koolaus underneath us and behind us, their stiff, perpendicular sides covered by mosses and trees. And, where the other side of the bowl began to climb again, there was the white of churches and houses and stores along the white strip of shoreline. Directly below us the old Pali road, closed now, was still visible. Paul's parents and grandparents would have traveled on it. A feat of engineering, it was opened in 1898. We could see Mount Olomana and the drive-in theater near the entrance to the winding, unlit road into the swamp. With effort, squinting against the light and fighting the furious Pali winds, we could even see our small house. Looking down, seeing the roof that must have been our own, we caught ourselves and sighed and felt our way in.

At the house the cat waited by the door as Paul unlocked it. "Hello Lukie. How's my baby cat?" I stooped to pick him up and stepped inside.

"Like it?" Paul touched the bones of my back lightly.

"Oh God. What'd you do?" It felt like someone else's house. I walked into the room uncertainly, a visitor.

Paul's voice behind me said, "Take off your shoes." Old joke. "You're not in Kansas any more."

But I stood still. I felt stupid and unreasonably afraid, like a blind woman in a room in which the position of every piece of furniture has been changed.

"You'll never believe how hard it was to get these mats in right," Paul said, still behind me. "You have to cut them and fit them, like making a pattern of the room. Then you have to sew the whole damn thing up...." I heard him drop the largest of my bags as if it added to his weariness, as if, unasked, he'd taken on the weight of redesigning our entire household and was unequal to the task.

"You know when a man gets rabies," Paul said, "he takes his house apart in the order he built it, only starting at the end...that's how they know—seeing him do what he did before only turned around...."

On the floor, fresh Chinese mats. New bookshelves on the wall by the glass doors. Outside there was an empty wire coat hanger on the be-still tree. A long paper lantern hung in one corner. Our furniture was rearranged. Some of it had been taken out completely. "Where's the old rocking chair—the one we shipped over with the clothes and the sewing machine?" A couple of things had been added from Revere. "We aren't supposed to have those," I said, nodding at them pointlessly. "Are we?" Paul knew the rules. "Those are Mihana's things." I turned around to look at him.

His thin shoulders in the habitual blue shirt were bending over to retrieve my bag. Nothing about him said what he'd done was a gift.

"A surprise," he mumbled.

"I just can't believe it." I started for our room, embarrassed by my pettiness. But the excitement and decisions had been his. And he hadn't asked about my father. Or how I felt.

Tilting and bumping behind me with the suitcase, he propelled me down the hall. In our room he dropped the bag once more with a soft thud on the new mats and sat down on the bed, looking me over. "So. How do you like it? Really?" Pleased with himself. Pulling his legs and bare feet up on the quilt. "C'mere," he said in his coaxing voice. He patted the empty space beside him.

"You never called me," I said.

I crossed the room nearing him, although we seemed to have dropped into a strange place, our lives and our surroundings rearranged in my absence. I took off my leis.

I sat down by him on the bed. That was the same. Even the sheets, as if he'd left them untouched, or had slept on them too carefully while I was gone. His arms pulled me down. I could feel the whole length of him when he kissed me. The press of his hand, darker than before, rose up in me like a memory.

"Mom!" Kit was calling me. She was testing the house. She went outside and came back in again, slamming the door, conferring with the cat. "Mom?"

Paul rolled away from me and groaned.

"Yes?" I called back, moving closer to him so that next to my eye I could see his hair, light as our daughter's, and the patches of skin on his nose and forehead that had repeatedly burned and peeled. My hand, beside me on the quilt, picked at a thread. I felt enlarged, my desire for him abnormal.

"Come see my room!" Beyond the wall, musing through her belongings, Kit concentrated on us.

In our room love threatened, his mouth covering mine and his hands coming up into my hair. "Lock the door," he said.

But I could not find the strength to stand up and shut the door and take off my clothes and enjoy those last, best minutes of my marriage. In our room time reappeared. "Wait till she goes to bed," I said. Then I got up and left him there.

SEVEN

In the morning, waking up late, I heard the mourning doves, their small claws on the tin roof over our lanai. I heard them speaking softly. I smelled flowers—not outside, but hanging on the lampshade where I'd left the leis. Tuberoses. A thick string of them, double weight—the white flowers interspersed with ferns, their sweet smell almost unbearable. Love mixed with regret. And everything came back to me. Our flight, the unfamiliar house. All night the smell of the flowers and, from the garden, sounds—as if things could be heard growing. This was Paul's favorite time of day and he had left the house. He would be having breakfast somewhere—he liked to eat breakfast at a neighborhood restaurant. Because of our distinct biologies, our inner rhythms, we'd managed over the years to miss each other's finer moments, as if our time zones didn't overlap. Why I slept through his mornings I don't know. What I did during the night hours when Paul and Kit were asleep, I don't remember. Sometimes I cleaned the house, looked at them in their beds. Perhaps I only walked through the dark rooms and listened to their breathing sounds. And always I enjoyed their sleeping. I kept watch. Without surprises, tucked into a place I tended nightly, they were mine.

That morning I got up, found Kit in the kitchen with the cat, and fixed my coffee, seeing, from the corner of my eye, the changes everywhere around me. Kit was eating cereal from a bowl on the floor. She had already made herself some pilot cracker and jelly sandwiches. There was evidence of grape jelly on her legs. I fixed two boiled eggs, taking them from a new brown fridge that was so big Paul had cut a wedge out of the counter top to fit it in. There was time now, and privacy, to sniff the house for difference, dog-prowling at the rooms, and I began my wanderings. Fingering books and toys in Kit's room with thoughts of where they'd come from, who had given them, on what occasion, I wondered why Paul had tampered with our nest. Childhood becomes selected memories: I always felt at home once I had entered Kit's child-room. But he had changed that too.

Kit was my link to magic. I seemed always to be urging her growth and at the same time throwing up barriers to her maturity. What I cherished most in her was the childishness of body. I loved her face for its wistful bone structure, its vegetarian expression. I regretted each lost tooth. I saved them in a box, watching the jaw angle itself, alarmed.

Now she ate her breakfast and played in her room, exhausted by the long passage. I did our laundry and sat with her, hurt by the room's lavender paint and the shelves I hadn't chosen for her wall. There was a pile of plastic lizards on her bed that she had left there through the night.

"I should have taken you along, I know," Kit whispered to her Snoopy dog, "but I forgot. I was so busy at the end." She took her Barbie dolls out of their shoe boxes and arranged them on her desk.

I went to the kitchen again. I watered one plant in the window, but it was damp already. The clock was wound. There was nothing to do but clean Kit's cracker crumbs off the floor and wait for Paul.

"Bring your suit and I'll take you on the boat," he said when he got back. He was speaking to Kit.

"I wish you took me with you today," she said to him.

He threw a six-pack of beer and a bottle of wine into the back seat, along with the camera and two or three lenses. The instrument was always with us. There was the time we capsized off Diamond Head and the plastic bag full of camera gear came unlashed when the boat flipped, green garbage bag floating off in one direction, Kit in her life-jacket floating off in another, the waves moving up and down, seesawing us, so that we all kept disappearing from sight and reappearing someplace else, directionless.

"The camera!" Paul yelled. As if all this buoyancy could be expected to obey.

Kit was disappearing, everything was disappearing. An enormous gravity of water pulled at my legs—I always think once I'm beyond the coastal shelf the downward drag of gravity is multiplied by depth—but I obeyed Paul and swam after the floating camera, terrified. He chased the boat down first, then came back for his child.

In the back seat now, the familiar things: Kit, the camera, the beer. In front, Paul driving, dressed in his jeans and a new Hawaiian shirt, nervous, taking us past the piled cars, the Lady on her tree, the stones of the temple hidden in the grass, to Lanikai, and to Revere with its great stone entrance and long drive, to the house where Maya and Mihana lived, where Maya had been born, and where their histories were as well hidden as all the treasures in the locked-up rooms, their secrets, like the furniture, under white sheets. Strange injuries had been inflicted there, it seemed to me, or Paul's own father wouldn't have cut himself off after the early death of his wife and disinherited his child.

The house. It fit into that perfect landscape perfectly. Weathered a silvery shade of green, it was the shell of a creature who had crawled away from it and left it huge and glittering, waiting, on the edge of the sea. Most of it was closed up. Most of the rooms were locked. Mihana and Maya lived in a small part of the house—two bedrooms, the sitting room, the kitchen, and the echoing hall.

Now Mihana's memories supported what was left of the place where Paul's maternal grandfather, Henry Needham, had made a fortune buying and selling sugar from his desk in the koa-paneled study and where Paul's mother, Julia Daniels Needham, had married her father's plantation manager, Hilton Quill; and where, her earthly work finished ahead of schedule, she had been laid to rest in some unmarked corner of the property. This was the house where Mihana had been raised and where Paul had lived until he'd been sent away to school.

Julia had left such clear instructions for the management of the house that nothing was ever modified—no chair moved, no recipe modernized, nothing replaced except by duplicate. But it was Hilton's will that had survived. It was his taste that was evident. He was a collector — of Chinese and Japanese antiques and Polynesian things—and what he'd chosen, including Mihana, what he'd placed in that house, was still there.

Mihana. How she has changed for me. Sometimes I cannot remember how she looked to me at first. Her long hair black and thick, worn down or braided under an old lauhala hat, her long muumuu fastened with a crescent-shaped bone pin. It was a lucky pin, she said. Her face was like no face I had known. There was in it, at the same time, benevolence and fury; there was an odd expression in it as if, within her, she combined beatitude and crime. All those wrinkled cotton coverings concealed a woman I couldn't understand—a mind that was old and tough and a body that was still soft, still in its prime. She radiated strength, as if at any moment she might change the weather or cause the ocean to rise.

As unpredictable as one of the mynah birds in Revere's banyan tree, Mihana filled the house with movement, flashing arms and hair and heat at everyone. She was in charge of the estate now and she applied herself to the place, directing her considerable energies at flowers, animals, and human hearts indiscriminately. But not Paul's. They had an odd relationship. They had been children together but Mihana had been more like a servant then. Paul's parents had called her their *hanai* child, which meant they'd taken her in. He used to say she'd have to die before we'd get Revere. He said she knew the legends of her people, and their fixes and cures, that she had dreams and visions, and that people who needed those things believed in her.

Now she appeared majestically to greet us, banging the door and stepping over her white dog to throw her arms around me. She was older than Paul by a few years—she must have been nearly forty—and larger, too, with energy to match. She smelled of dogs and dirt and hair pomade. She had been digging in the garden, scraping away at it—there was a line of blue earth under her nails and a lei around Julia's old lauhala hat. She wore her customary muumuu which was immense, but she filled it easily. Mihana was large-bodied and over six feet tall, and I felt diminished and protected and encompassed by her.

"So," she said, inspecting me, standing back and then putting a heavy arm around me again. "So. You look okay. But thin. Plenty thin! Kit, kiss your auntie. Tell me about your trip. How come you wiggling so much? You have to make *shi-shi* the first second you're here again?" From somewhere, she produced two unruly leis for us, a mix of jungle flowers and greenery. "Where did Paul run off to?" She brushed our faces with her cheek and held me against her bulk. Paul had disappeared. He had slipped off to the seductive beach, where the sun was angled against the lapping tide, down across the lawn and behind the ironwood trees and toward the boat. Kit, freed by Mihana, was running off after him. Mihana was pulling me through the thumping dogs. I felt a little surge of hope and for some reason thought of my aunts. My father was dead but once again I was being taken in hand.

The house suggested an accommodation to abuse that I could never put my finger on. Something was wrong there, as if an anguish had come in and settled over it at some point in the past. Built by Paul's grandfather on Julia's side, it stood close to the ocean on good Hawaiian land, a pie slice stretching over five acres from the shore to the cliffs. Paul's grandfather had used it as a beach retreat, so I doubted that it was his misery that oppressed the place. It was Julia who had turned it into a home. The hallway, as wide as a room and very long with windows down the sides, connected several rooms and separate structures, as if none of it had been planned. It was a passageway in the original sense— a place to be conveyed along—but it had koa chests, plain-cut and polished golden brown, and faded oriental rugs running the length of it. It was a passageway to all the small, locked rooms surrounding it.

At the far end it opened to a low-ceilinged sitting room, the only public place in a house built around private sympathies, dense with old flowered furniture and dust. Off to one side in the unused study, piled books and papers sat on the untouched shelves where they had been left by Hilton, as if at any moment he might return. On his desk was a carved bust covered in silk. The cloth was carefully knotted at the throat, but features were vaguely discernible under it. No one had ever unveiled it. Old photographs in gilt frames leaned against each other on various surfaces. There was a wooden filing cabinet and a bookcase and a secretary as well as the desk. All these were covered with pictures but there were only two family photographs. Over the lintel of the door a motto had been carved by a mocking hand: *Abandon innocence you who enter here.* Small artifacts were everywhere, thin pieces of Hawaii's past. Hilton had married into this house—a middle-aged businessman, judging by the 1930s sepia-colored print that rested on his desk. He was almost fifty when he married. And next to him was Julia, not of his own kind, it would seem, but pale and wan, her straight hair covered by a hat—the same one Mihana wore now. She was thirty-eight when Paul was born. There were no pictures of Paul anywhere. As if he can't exist, I thought, as if Hilton and Julia never touched at all, never got married, never got into bed. This part of the great beach house, once open to the wide lanai, a typical island porch protected from the rain and sun by a deep double-pitched red tile roof, was closed and dark now and smelled of the sea.

The sitting room had long windows that let in the light, except that the bamboo blinds were always drawn, giving a filtered look to everything—to the poi pounders, wooden calabashes, pieces of porcelain and teak and bone and jade, the valuable things Hilton had bought or saved. They looked a little out of place on Julia's English furniture. Neither culture seemed quite at peace, in fact. Books and plates and pictures, wooden images and things made of feather and stone—all of them were uneasy here.

When I sat down on the flowered sofa, Mihana exhaled as if she were connected to the room. "Something to drink?" She still wore the hat.

"I guess iced tea." The choice here was the special tea she made or Primo beer.

"So. Well. You're back exactly when?" She was still standing at the entrance to the room, staring back in. She often repeated things. "About your father, Jess. It's too bad. Too bad."

On a card table there was a brochure lying on a pile of magazines: *Should Man Control Evolution?* And a paperback, *Ka Po'e Kahiko, The People of Old.*

"Paul has completely changed our house," I told her, looking discreetly around the room, looking for holes and vacancies. Behind each picture, under each object in the room, there was probably clean, virgin wood, a whole shade lighter than the room I saw, as if time had been trapped in shapes and pieces there. "What is right for mankind?" the brochure asked in large black lettering. Hilton's photographs—a valuable collection of early Hawaiian scenes—leaned out from the walls.

Paul's father had bought every photograph of the islands in the old days that he could find. Having been born on the mainland, it was as if he had wanted to purchase membership in the race. I studied the pictures he had put on the damp, salty walls, pictures with titles imprinted or scratched on them in ink: Hawaiian Woman with Brooch, Hawaiian Days, Hawaiian Girl with Long Hair and long, level gaze. Punahou College at Honolulu. Riding the Surf at Waikiki, the beckoning arm of the Moana Pier, long gone, still a blur in front of Diamond Head so that the crater seemed to have a set of underwater legs, to be geologically unsound. Nuuanu Pali, the old road, a quarter-rim around the cup of the windward plain, the photograph showing only the edge, a few feet of flattened earth, and below, the moonlike abyss of gray, as if the planet there still lay untouched.

A Date Palm Avenue. A building, formerly the King's Palace. Queen Kapiolani. Queen Kalama. Native Flower Girls—who sit on the ground in high-necked dresses for ever, long, untied leis hanging on the wall behind them, like ropes. Oahu Sugar Mill. Waikiki Beach.

Mihana disappeared and I lay back and waited. The time that was trapped here was Hilton's time, everything the way he had left it on whatever day or month or year he had last put it there. Except for the brochure and magazines. Abandon innocence you who enter here. I would leave my indentation on the sofa when I stood up, but nothing else. An antique copy of *Omai, First Polynesian Ambassador to England* lay on a table next to a wing-backed chair, marked by a ribbon that protruded from its side. Maybe Hilton had been sitting there reading it ten years ago, the night he died. I opened it:

By the time Cook's ships had dropped anchor, two or three thousand native men and girls had reached them by

*canoe and by swimming and were all swarming aboard the
floating temples....*

Upstairs in a room I hadn't seen, Mihana had a tiny library full
of Christian texts, books of Victorian poetry, books on music,
painting, and gardening. Most of the pages were uncut. She knew
what she knew, she had said once, before she came to this house.
"The rest here, if I like it, I memorize. It hurts my eyes to read
too much. I like to go over and over things." Her palms up,
shrugging. "Until I know exactly what they mean."

Hearing her in the hallway, I sat up and called out, "Where's
Maya anyway?"

"Out with the kids." She put a glass of beer on the card table
in front of me, obviously thinking I needed it more than tea, and
walked across the room to peer outside. Paul and Kit always
will be kids to her, while I'm from far away and suspected of a
lack of innocence. The local word for "white" is *haole*, meaning
outsider; and mainland *haole* is by far the worst.

"So," I said, reaching for my foggy glass.

Mihana turned to look at me. Then she said, "You go first. First
you tell me." She straightened up to her full height.

"Not much to say." I crossed my legs, and put the beer glass
down again. I had a skirt on and I was glad. In front of her I
always felt exposed.

"There is. There is."

"What?"

"Plenty to say."

"When I got there he was dead." But I was thinking of Revere.
Of sitting on the bare lanai, hands on my knees like a sentinel,
protecting it. Waiting for time to come back to it, to move back
in. I would hire a gardener. I would put Paul's pictures on the
walls. The one of Maya in my dress and shawl—dressing up
with Kit. The one of my bare feet. Plenty of Kit. That one of the
old man walking in Manoa Valley. I might even, I thought, paint

the walls white and lighten the house. But nothing else. My long-lost father. Come home and dead. There was nothing I could tell Mihana.

"We used to stick the spirit back in the body through the feet," she said.

"I never got to see him." For a moment my voice cracked.

But she finished. "All the same then. Nothing changed from before. But something else occurred." Mihana lifted her hands as if conferring a benediction. The hat was tilted, almost covering an eye. "Are you worrying? What's on your mind?"

Something was on *her* mind, I thought, no doubt about it, and everyone else had had the good sense to be somewhere else. I tried to prepare myself. Paul claimed she didn't live entirely in the here and now. Around us were the ancient articles of an old faith. They were things Hilton had collected. But they were hers now.

"The wind is perfect for the boat. You want to go out?" She stretched lazily. "Or stay with me?"

"I'm actually kind of tired. I'm probably jet-lagged and I didn't get much sleep."

"Maybe because of going home. The past can be a sad place. What was it like there this time?"

"It's a normal house, close to the tracks in a Kansas town." Each room of that small house, full of recollections and images, was too cramped, too congested to have room for me. It was a skin I'd shed. It was the place I had been lying, under a window, stretched out in the sun, the first time I'd felt my breasts tender against the floor and known I was leaving my childhood. I had felt like Orpheus, leaving behind me all that beauty. That house was the only place, until this island, in my life's complex geography, where my dreams knew their way around.

I adjusted my skirt. It was a wrap-around—something women wore a lot at that time—and it was bunched up under me. "As far as my mother goes, maybe we think the same but she's had a hard time."

"And," Mihana purred, "you feel better here, in this house?"

I shrugged.

But she looked anxious. "Then I will tell you what happened," she said quickly, leaping over the preliminaries, "in that case." I could tell by her look it was going to be one of her "dreams". I lifted the antique book on the table by the wing chair and glanced at it, wishing Paul would come back. Omai: First Ambassador.... The true story of his voyage there in 1774 with Captain Cook; of how he was fêted by Fanny Burney, approved by Samuel Johnson, entertained by Mrs. Thrale and Lord Sandwich, and painted by Sir Joshua Reynolds. Suffered and was buried.

"You want to come upstairs?"

"What have you been up to?" I asked, suddenly polite, to forestall whatever was coming. "While I was home. The garden?"

"The same. The same." Her way of emphasizing things was to repeat them. "I look after this place. And Maya. Nothing else. Except for the *heiau* in the swamp—I'm working on it now—close to your house. Ulupo's the name of it."

"What do you do there?"

Mihana looked down modestly. "Maybe I can fix it a little bit. That was a sacred place," she announced, shaking her head at me as if I were to blame for the suburb around it, " an old settlement built on a bay that is now only swamp and trash. There's a strong *kapu* there of course but nobody takes care of it."

"How do you know what to do?" I wondered if she had fixed our dinner ahead of time. She had not mentioned it and I was tired and hungry. Instead she was turning to look outside again through the blinds which were still at half-mast. "You can figure out how it used to be?" I said.

She took a deep, patient breath. "My belief is the voyagers landed there. It makes sense to me. I mean the first ones. The very first settlers. My ancestors. They call them *menehunes* now. You know? Meaning little people. Magic people. Supposed to come out at night and make things—*heiaus* and fishponds in the reef. With stone. Build walls and all that kind of thing. You see? They weren't little or magic. They were just like me. Everywhere it's the same. When the next group of voyagers came with new gods they used that story to diminish the old ones. You have to make the ones you conquer small in some way, change the gods or just plain throw them away. The new people brought Kukealimoku— we call him Ku, a warrior god. But this *heiau* was for Lono, the Old One. They send him away but sometimes he comes back for a short while during his season. There was a ceremony. He brought fertility and rain. That kind of thing."

"Kit studied that at school. The kids still reenact that ceremony every year. They do everything, make their own tapa cloth and carry this crosspiece draped in white. They collect canned goods in a net and give them away to the poor. The *heiau* was for him?"

"Not recently. This *heiau* is *pau* a long time back. It is exceedingly old." Her voice moved melodically around certain words. Ex-ceed-ing-ly. Odd pidgin phrases mixed with the kind of Victorian English that must have been spoken by Julia or Hilton here.

I leaned back and stretched my legs, as if I were still cramped, still on an airplane moving slowly, insignificantly, between one place and another. "You could get helpers. Students. Researchers. Is it public property?"

Mihana leaned back too. She had forgotten to tell me "what happened". Instead she was in a story-telling mood, and I was relieved.

"They concentrate on rocks. Maybe what counts is af-fin-ity."

"Maybe." Affinity. The Hawaiians say that in the life of the land is the preservation of righteousness. I wondered how it would feel to believe in something larger than my household and gave way to a little spate of philosophic jealousy. To make up for it I said, "This is the god they got mixed up with Captain Cook, is it?"

Mihana shrugged. "He is," she agreed. "Oh, maybe he came back even before that too. He said he'd return on a floating island with tall trees." She seemed to relax for the first time that afternoon, and looked up at the dark ceiling, then down at her feet. I relaxed too, thinking she had forgotten whatever it was she'd meant to talk to me about. I was afraid it might be part of her other world, half-dreamlike and half visionary, and I would not know how to respond or what to say. But Mihana, in a certain mood, loved to "talk story", and now she was settling in, moving her thighs apart expansively, dipping her right hand in the air as if testing it.

"He arrived from the horizon on that im-mense ship with those e-nor-mous masts with all their branches and hanging cloth. Imagine seeing such a thing for the first time looming up out of the ocean and the sky. Imagine being brought up on a promise that has finally come true. Of course he comes in other guises. Certainly!" She smiled to herself. "But just imagine standing in a soft bark skirt, holding a large gourd in your arms or *hala* leaves or taro roots. Never mind. Think of never seeing such a foreign thing — so fantastic and amazing — never before. Never in all the chants except the one that promises this god. Imagine standing there watching him stepping out into the shallow water. People are shouting out the name. *O Lono....*" Here Mihana roared a little for my benefit. "It happens to be his season! Festivities to call him back are even in progress. His staff is carried clear around each island by his priest. Now he arrives! There he is in a long cloak with a strange helmet on his head. His skin has ornaments, colors and stripes. Lono is from a distant place. He comes to conquer Ku, the warrior god. Everyone wants his *mana*. Each family. He lies with the daughter of the ruling house. This way his *mana* will be taken in by her and given back to us in the form of his child.

71

"Then finally"— Mihana waved the hand which had been keeping time to her story and, in Hawaiian fashion, illustrating it—"finally after a few months his sojourn with us is done. He doesn't want to go but all the food which has been saved in anticipation of his arrival is eaten up. You see? First we are calling out his name, flinging ourselves down at his feet, wrapping him in a sacred feather cape, taking him to the *heiau*, feeding him sacred things. Taking care of his men. The girls want to sleep with them. Their bodies also contain treasure. This is the reason, after the *haoles* come, they swim out to visiting ships year after year. Looking for foreign strength. It isn't naughtiness, this lust, it is beyond all that. The girls are looking for the lost god's divinity. Of course such generosity puts a strain on things. There is no work, only sports and lovemaking and games. Captain Cook sails off on the exact day his festivities are over, according to the priests. But he has trouble with his ship and turns back. The warrior god is back in the place of honor. Captain Cook is a trespasser now. He cannot be Lono now. He breaks the *kapu*. To break the *kapu* requires human sacrifice. You see? After poor Captain Cook is killed, after he's struck and falls into the shallow water of the bay, some of his bones are carried to his ship."

Mihana dropped her hand and paused dramatically. "The people carrying the bones have one question. They ask it of the English as they are handing the wrapped bones up the steep-sided ship. 'When will he come again?' they ask. But the English do not answer back."

When Mihana stopped, I heard a bird call out and the wind swept through the large crisp leaves of banana trees outside. I thought about the first people from my world to find this place, and how it must have looked to them. Small huts around huge temples and the enormous ocean that surrounded everything. I thought about the canoes that long before had struck out from the Marquesas and landed on the edge of a great sunken crater, an uninhabited world. They carried gods and plants and animals on those canoes. "How long ago was it?" I said.

"Was what? 1778."

"No. That *heiau*." I was thinking about the destruction she might wreak on the last evidence of her history. "How can you be sure how the stones should go?"

"I remember a few things...bits of *mele*, the chants, from my mother even. The words for the ceremonies. The position of things. I would say, to answer your question, Jesse, it's been there since the fourth century anyway. That's how old the stuff is they been digging up on Molokai, up in Halawa Valley."

My stomach growled. "If I went to the kitchen could I...."

Mihana heaved herself up, placing a small hand on each arm of her chair. "You could help me," she agreed. "Follow please."

I stood up gratefully as she went toward the hall. She was leading the way, as if she had wanted to move in the direction of the kitchen all along. "Another beer maybe," I put in, "while we cook."

"Not yet." She made a quick turn to the right—a turn that took her to the foot of her stairs. "But bring your glass."

Suddenly, a great reluctance. But she took my hand. Soberly, almost grimly, as if she had something important to show me, her hand even smaller than I expected, gentler, she led me up the narrow tube of stairs from the long hallway to what she called her quarters, the only upstairs room—a kind of perch—in the whole house.

"I want to tell you something," she said, panting a little, the stairs sinking beneath her. We entered her room. She went to an enormous chair that was carved and decorated like a canoe, and stood next to it, touching my arm very gently and then releasing it.

"This thing was so unusual," she said, closing her eyes and shading them with a hand. "It was not the kind of dream I have. It was more than that." Mihana's face was like the earth. It was earth-colored and now it looked earth-worn. She could have been fifty, a hundred years old.

I shifted from one foot to another, already apprehensive and out of place. I waited for her to offer me a chair. Without looking, hand still over her eyes, she pointed. "Sit down. Sit down."

In a corner there was an old bookcase with heavy glass doors that contained her library. Mihana slept in a heavy four-poster bed strung with an old mosquito net. I backed into a hard, upright chair. I noticed everything; I had never been invited to her room upstairs before. I noticed the objects on her dresser, the books and papers on her desk, a necklace in a Chinese bowl, and, on the floor, layers of lauhala mats that smelled like damp straw.

"This occurred around sunset," her voice tolled, the trade winds blowing her words past me so that I leaned forward to hear what she said. "Two weeks ago. I was in here. In this room. Listening to my radio and preparing some things, looking through my windows a little. I was having my glass of water. You know. Then I sat down." She looked past me. Her words sounded clipped, formal and distant from normal speech, but her voice was musical and I felt myself falling into it.

"Yes." I knew the water she referred to was more likely gin. She was a follower of the goddess Pele, or so Paul said.

"And then it happened. I dreamed this thing. Should I keep it to myself? Or tell it privately? Maybe to you. Because it seems to me a personal dream. Involving my own child. Also a warning."

"Maya?" I said.

Outside I could hear the small, sharp chink chink chink of a metal stay against a mast and the sharp tight snap of a sail. Looking through Mihana's window, which was of thick glass almost opaque with imbedded salt, I saw our sail, a dim shape going past, and Maya's small dark head in front of it. Her head was thrown back and she leaned over the water horizontally. A Hobie Cat is almost Hawaiian in design. It has two hulls, which makes it a true catamaran, and between and over them a large canvas trampoline laced down the center like a piece of cloth that has been torn open and then laced up with giant string.

Without warning, Mihana's eyes narrowed and rolled back. She lapsed into a kind of chant, throwing her head back and thrusting one hand out in front of her. "The first that I see, your hair is blowing like a wind—your face is like the moon with eyes of stone. She holds her small breast in her hand—I see her body like a flower"—here Mihana sagged and drew in a breath, then struck up again—"I know her heart is double-edged, it wounds what it desires to defend. I see a fine koa canoe—the water rises and pulls back. The water breaks the boat in two and a child is floating like a leaf. I stand above the water and the trees—Dress the infant, a voice says—keep it dry—then you lean down into the current. I lift the child who has eyes of a shark. I dress the child in a vine."

Mihana slowly opened her eyes. After a moment, in a normal voice, she said, "this dream is very clear. This one is a warning dream."

"This was about Maya?"

"Some was about you."

"Is that all of it?" I asked. "*Pau*?"

"Do you know what it's about?" She looked up at me.

"Not really." I was embarrassed for us both. I shook my head. "This is a warning?" I said, forcing a tone of credulity into my voice. I tried to sound logical. "Why would that be?"

A thick twilight was dropping over us, brought by a clatter of mynah birds dropping into the banyan tree and squawking as they found their branches for the night. Kit and Paul and Maya were still out on the Hobie Cat, catching the last wind of this wasted day.

"It must be awful to have dreams like that," I said, lamely, over the shrieks outside. "If you believe in them."

Mihana frowned as if I hadn't been listening, and had missed the point. She heaved herself out of the chair as if the effort of retelling her dream had drained her. Then she drifted past me, through the door and down the quaking stairs.

I sat there in the darkening room, listening to the birds, waiting for the sudden silence that always comes when they have settled things among themselves. They had rushed up to the sky to find the night, and after their squabbling they would pull it over us like a ticking warmth.

In this room the everlasting salt spray of the ocean just outside had turned the furniture dull gray, and the sand of Lanikai, finest and whitest in all the world, had sifted into every cranny and mingled with the dust of every surface. Now I was left alone, trusted with all Mihana's privacy. This was the part of Revere I didn't know.

She had come from a plantation on the north shore where Hilton had been *luna*—manager. We all knew that. She had come as a companion for Paul who was four or five years younger, or to be raised by *haoles*, or for her own good, come for reasons that remained unclear, but she had been raised in this house, right here. And finally she had inherited it. I wondered if she knew how much Paul cared.

I heard Mihana's voice. I followed it and her fading footsteps downstairs.

"You think it was about one of us?" I asked a few minutes later, setting my empty beer glass on a counter. "Your warning?"

We were in the kitchen, where Mihana had begun a ponderous dance between enormous tables, giant sinks, and stoves, knowing the whole stage perfectly, her hands turning dainty at the prospect of a meal. I set my glass down on a white-tiled counter. With one hand she was chopping four large cucumbers with a cleaver, while with the other she opened the screen door and reached outside to clip ti-leaves which she would wrap around the fish before it was baked. She was a good cook, knowing the chemistry of things, but she stopped her clattering and chopping for a minute and stood still, facing me. Then she turned back to the food.

"If I dream of wearing a feather cloak. Suppose." The cleaver slammed something under her hand. "If I am rich, this means I will be poor. But if I am poor, it means the opposite. I come from voyagers. When my people, called the Kena, came we brought our way of seeing things. A warning comes with the canoe. To me this canoe is an important thing." A giant ti-leaf seemed to explode in front of her. Pieces of it flew up and landed close to me.

Watching the kitchen darken around her preparations, the white dog rubbing against us, and Mihana, between steps, crouching over it and fondling its ears, I had no thought for the afternoon melt of beach outside, stretched like a long girl with Paul in wet arms. I picked a shiny ti-leaf up and held it. The air had softened and I must have heard the muted thud of the boat against the sand behind Mihana's voice. But I was pulled into her tuneless murmuring, a tuneless song that she was singing to herself.

Suddenly Kit was in the doorway and, within moments, Paul, then Maya. Beautiful Maya, woman-child. Turning in her years like the moon in a spring landscape, Maya reflected any light around her. She was accessible and remote at the same time. She was fourteen. She was all angles and all grace, all breast and bone, stomach and knee. She was quick and deceptive, she was candid and shy, she was equally smart and naive, and her appearance in the kitchen was unsettling to each of us in some degree. She came across the floor and put her arms around my waist. "My *keiki*," said her mother gazing fondly. "Little *lehua*. Maya."

One minute she was Mihana's sweet lehua flower and the next Mihana would be shouting, "Out of here with that bubblegum!" And Maya would be tucking it under the lip of a koa table and turning the volume up on her tiny transistor radio. Soon she would retrieve the gum, put it back in her busy mouth, and start a hula, leading us down the hall, shuffling her bare feet as if she wore a sweeping gown, as if she were a princess which, indeed, a hundred years ago, according to the bloodlines we could trace, she might have been.

She would lie down wherever she was, right on the floor in front of us. Like an animal, she'd fall asleep at our feet. Sometimes she would sit for hours, dreamy and almost still, only a leg tossing in the air like a wing, as if she'd alighted and might depart at any moment. Later she'd swoop through the rooms of Revere unstrung. She'd have her little transistor radio in her hand, a plug in one ear to keep peace with Mihana. Mihana would laugh. "Watch her." And we would. We'd watch her moving to the silent music in brown, unironed shorts and a small T-shirt.

When she came to our house, Maya and Kit tried on my makeup, dressing in my clothes and shoes. They had a game called "Shoes" which involved a different dance, a different promenade for each pair. They bathed together, plastering their hair into shapes with shampoo: Hey, how's this one? Hey, is this me? Then wild chortles. It was already there, visible in the bones under Maya's perfect skin—the woman she would be. It was close enough, almost, this coming beauty that was hers, to touch. She put her hair up and took it down. She moved from child to woman in an afternoon. Opening wooden louvers, letting in light, turning herself into a princess or a goddess for an afternoon with Kit; sometimes the two of them would concoct a play and then perform it for us at night. A curtain would be thrown up around an antique bed or across the narrowest neck of the hall and we would be instructed to sit on the floor to watch an entire show, including station breaks and news items that sounded like Maya's radio.

"Hey, what you doing all wet in the kitchen, you?" Maya was suddenly laughing, squeezing Kit from behind and grabbing her wet hair in both hands to wring it out over a sink. Kit screamed and wiggled out of her grasp, excited, as we all were, by this uncommon gathering in this uncommon place.

Paul pulled me aside. He held me for a minute, brushing the palm of his hand along my spine. He had showered in the old bath house and smelled of Mihana's homemade shampoo. "Let's forget that party if you want. It's already late." He released me and threw his towel on the back of a chair. "Smells good!" he said to Mihana in a louder voice; he was smiling at her.

I shrugged. "I don't mind the party."

Paul's smile faded. "You want to? You sure?"

Kit ran outside to find her lei and the rest of us filed into the dining room, Paul carrying the bottle of red wine he'd retrieved from the back seat of the car. Maya placed herself at the end of the table opposite her mother and called for order, making a joke of this small feast, as if she had an announcement, and Paul leaned across to pour her a glass of wine.

"No wine for that one," Mihana said, pointing at Maya's glass. She took her hat off for the first time and threw it on an empty chair, her hair tumbling down.

Following her arm, Paul and I turned, and I remembered the first time we had met on the beach over a charcoal fire and how we had been drawn to her long, childish, wild grace. Now she took a wad of bubblegum from her mouth and stuck it to the bottom of her glass so Paul couldn't lift it. "So?" she said.

Mihana refused wine for herself as well. "Why don't you go get me a beer," she pouted. "You know I don't like that stuff. And don't give me a hard time, eh Paul?" She drew her shoulders up.

Kit had come back to the table. I sent her back to the kitchen for the beer.

"Now I have my family," Mihana declared pouring the pale foaming liquid into her glass. Then she raised it. We all drank. She said, "And a toast to Kit, who brings Auntie Mihana a little something to sip on. Here's a milk toast!"

Kit took a large gulp of milk.

Paul had told me about leaving Revere, his father driving him to the pier with Mihana in the back seat of the car to say goodbye to him. "There were hula dancers by the ships back then," he had said, "and a band and streamers. It was a big deal, those ships going out and coming in. And Mihana walked me down. She took care of me. She was my best friend."

Paul poured himself another glass of wine, and one for me. I seemed to be swallowing too fast. He made a toast I don't remember. Something about the women around him. He was outnumbered by us, four to one. He was pleased. His eyes, at the end of the table, shining with pleasure, flustered me.

"Eat your good food I made you!" Mihana commanded, waving her arm over our plates. "And who's saying grace? I almost forgot. Let us join hands. You better say it, *keiki*."

But Maya shook her head. "No, I don't want to."

I looked at Paul and at the room around him, as if it belonged to a real, functioning house. Something about the place made Paul more confident and the rest of us sat straighter as if we'd taken on historic postures, as if Paul's grandparents and parents were with us in the room. Paul's mother had been a child in this house. So had Mihana and then Paul for a few years. Maya was raised here too. But it was no place for a childhood. Kit in her tall, straight chair looked overwhelmed. If she had spilled her milk, the ghosts of Julia and Hilton would have risen from the floor.

We joined hands. "Kit?" I said.

Kit bowed her head, making a face only I could see. "The one from school?... God is great God is good let us thank Thee for our food amen."

Maya was playing with her food. She was looking down at one of Julia's English plates and moving the piece of ham her mother had given her around on it with her fork. She began tearing it into pieces with her fingers making different shapes, arranging them. A dog. A tree.

"Did you tell Maya about your dream?" I asked, but Mihana frowned and Paul broke in. He said, "Jess and I have a party later on. Remember I told you, Maya?" He caught her eye. "So can you come back with us and watch Kit?"

Maya dropped her hands and rubbed a napkin between her fingers as if the request required thought. It seemed to me that Kit could do with a sitter who lived closer to the house, but Paul wasn't ready to agree, and we didn't go out much in the evening anyway.

Maya was staring past us into the windows, into the banyan tree. Mihana leaned forward and inclined an ear toward her daughter. For some reason, everyone waited. Paul sat motionless and Kit stopped chewing and fell silent. Then Maya nodded and we all relaxed, making squeaky sounds with our chairs as we shifted in them.

"We oughta fix these screens," Paul said, swatting an arm.

Standing up suddenly, Maya left the room with a large bone from the ham and we soon heard the snarls of the dogs forced to fight over one indivisible, coveted treat. Kit ran after her and Paul excused himself and left the room.

We'd eaten fish, cold ham, breadfruit, and yams. Macaroni salad. Poi. We had already had too much to drink and I felt tired and sick. Mihana walked me down the long hall toward the door, checking her gestures in the mirrors and windows luminous against the night. I hadn't offered to help her clear the table. In this house we were treated as honored guests, and that seemed only fair, considering. She whispered in my ear, "You coming to play Scrabble with me one day soon?"

In the deep tropical grass that fringed the darkest part of Julia's garden, Mihana's dog raced with its shadow, white hound against dark hound, blending into the shadows cast by the ancient monkey pods and banyan tree.

"You come see me for Scrabble," Mihana nodded, staring out. "We'll play. And talk."

I listened for Paul. "You always win."

"No. Never mind. You come. We have to talk. It was about Paul too, that dream." She put her hand gently on the back of my neck. She was pressed against me. I could feel her heat and see the drops of moisture that had just appeared around her mouth. I could feel her breath. "If a canoe is broken....This means a warning, Jesse Quill. Maybe a death in the family. Maybe."

I'd already had one of those. But under her hand my hair rose very slightly on the back of my neck. Her voice was so dolorous. The dog was still chasing something invisible under the huge trees. And there was the dream itself. But I heard Paul and the girls getting into the car. "Thank you for telling me," I said.

EIGHT

The slippers and sandals littering our host's doorway were as anonymous and various as flowers and we left ours with them. The art gallery was downstairs. Paul's photographs were still hanging there. The door was open. The stereo was furious. A joint was being passed among the guests. They were standing and sitting around the floor, long skirts and muumuus spread around them, bare feet, bottles of beer. Some of them looked up at us. There were stiff jokes and musical requests. Paul was already stepping across the legs and plates and bottles and someone handed him a beer. I edged my way into the crowded room.

Photo talk. "...I use slides, but either's okay."

There was no one I knew there except Paul. Paul had his hand out right and left, shaking other hands, accepting compliments, receiving kisses on his cheek. He had moved us here without a job, with nothing but his camera and his family name, wanting a new identity. Instead of commercial work he wanted to be known for the kind of work he did best. He wouldn't get paid as much but there was still the allowance from the trust.

Inside the racial cocktail of this gathering there was the usual undercurrent of anti-*haole*, anti-mainland bias I had encountered at every social event on the island. It ran through the room sluggish and cold, but everyone knew it was there and waded around it, covering it with courtesy. In one corner there was a conversation in heavy pidgin. They were all locals. No way to break in. Because the Hawaiian race in its pure form is gone, local means any race or mixture. It indicates only where you were born.

Paul had been given a lei. They liked him here. His pictures were taken seriously. He sidled up to me. "Hey, what's the problem? You know some of these people. Some of them at least. Don't you? You've seen them around with me."

"I'm fine."

"Here's our host!" said Paul, grabbing a man by the arm. He greeted me formally, although Paul had interrupted him in the act of showing someone his collection of contemporary and prehistoric art. He didn't call it prehistoric art, he called it pre-contact art, stabbing at the air with one hand and, with the other, squeezing the arm of a long-haired Chinese girl who stood listening to his proclamations as if they were convincing her. I had seen him look me over when I paused just inside his door.

Paul joined my hand to the one that had been stabbing the air, and introduced us. Either I didn't hear his name or I forgot it instantly.

"Just make yourself happy," the host instructed us, dropping my hand. He still gripped the girl. He had coal-black and gray hair. He was part Hawaiian, maybe part Japanese. "Just go ahead." Over his shoulder, "I've got to turn things over on the grill and keep the big guys from eating everything all up." He sounded nervous and effeminate. Someone edged past us with a plate of something hot. Carnival smell. The good host vanished. "I think he likes my work," said Paul, eyeing the plate.

"Pork," said a voice.

"Turn down the tube."

"He runs a magazine here too." Paul spoke around his food. "He makes most of his money on it."

"Chicken."

"For you," another woman with black hair said, putting a second lei around Paul's neck and kissing him. "He's beautiful," she added for my benefit. "I love the floating rocks. And the girl. The one in the shawl."

Paul introduced us. "Hi," she breathed. "You're his wife? Oh yes. How nice. You're pregnant? *Hapai?*"

I sucked my stomach in. Vaguely apologetic, I shook my head. Our host was circling the room. Outside his tiki torches burned. Inside candles and incense and marijuana smoke muddied the air. "They're masks," he crowed loudly to someone, indicating the old Hawaiian war helmets on his wall. There were two of them, made of gourds, and they glowered at us with round, empty eyes.

"You wanna hit?" The room was full of smoke. Everyone was suspended in an exotic gloom. A joint was passed.

Paul ambled off with the black-haired woman and I picked up his beer pretending to be headed for the food. There was a long report from the TV in the corner, which could be heard around the music and food and conversation, about the war in Vietnam. War and babies, I thought. The big moments in our lives. A man goes off to kill or doesn't. A woman has a child or doesn't. That's how we take charge of life and death and time.

"Jesus. Look at that." They were counting bodies. There were statistics. Someone turned the TV off.

"Now let's see," said my host to someone, stacking some small skewers of meat on the grill. He seemed to be talking to himself. It was quieter outside, almost empty on the little porch behind his kitchen. "You're the one who just moved here a little while back. You missed Paul's show." I had joined him because I was hungry again and there was no one to talk to inside. I couldn't remember his name but at least we had been introduced. "You're with Paul." He wiped his hands. "Grandson of Henry Needham. Son of Hilton Quill. That your old man? Quite a lineage. Kind of a *kamaaina* but not quite an old-timer though."

"He was born here."

"I know. I know. You need something. I can tell. What would you like? You can tell me, I'm your host." He glanced at the beer I was holding, Paul's beer.

"Another drink. A place to sit down...." I nodded at the barbecue he was tending. "Those smell good."

"Why bother with a place to sit when I have a floor and a bed and you already have a drink?"

"Your floor is covered by respectable ladies," I said. He must have been older because of the hair. His face was pocked. But nice. "I don't know about your bed." He was missing a couple of teeth on one side.

"But I have no idea what you can be talking about." Mock horror. "I do not invite respectable ladies to my home." I was on safe ground. This was a meaningless seduction. We were only wasting a little time.

"It's the real Hawaiian I'm trying to get," someone said. I turned around. There was a small, languid group on the porch steps having an earnest discussion. They were lounging against the rails.

"There's no prescription though, man. Not out here. It takes trust. They're primitive. I mean in the best meaning of the word. They still believe in things."

"You take pictures. You might as well put up a hotel. You're still using them."

"Soul stealing? Bullshit."

"Your husband—is he your husband?—makes good pictures." My host was making conversation with me now. "What...do you do?"

"Nothing," I said. I was a wife and mother. I believed in myself as far as that went but to this man I was just another wife. I was nothing in his eyes. In marriage, my mother had said, your role is nothingness. This is your natural state. You are the smile, the cure, the medicine. So I was primitive in my own way. I believed, in those days, in my own passivity. I believed it was good for my family. "Nothing," I said again.

He wasn't listening. "I hang a new show day after tomorrow. Tapa cloth. Do you want to see the deck? I'll take you. It's my latest pride. You tell me where you've been, before you got here. We'll walk around my house together. I'll even show you the tapa cloth if you want. I don't mean where you've been tonight. I mean all your life."

"Just say this is Kansas, where I come from." I made an X at my wrist and ran my index finger up my arm. "Two years in Colorado. One year in Arizona." I crooked my elbow. "A summer in Mexico. Mostly in Mazatlan. Santa Fe. A few other places. I forget the names. Now we've settled in though. We're into a second year."

"But you went away again."

"My father died." I said this almost proudly.

"Very heavy," he said. "Anyway"— he was trying to change the subject—"now you're settled in."

Except for the languid conversation on the steps, there was no one around us. He dug a beer out of the tub at his feet and opened it smoothly, knocking its cap against the edge of the grill.

From the porch I heard "...surfing accident."

I peered through the window next to me. Paul had disappeared. He was gregarious at parties. No matter how futile they were.

My host sipped at his beer. "You need something?" he said again. His hand, after its immersion in ice water, looked innocent and clean.

"What I need is another drink. I just got back yesterday." I followed my host, whose name I didn't know, to a shelf he had built around one side of his property, the side that fell away. The shelf was balanced on stilts.

The porch was behind us now, a remnant of the party and the kitchen door and the barbecue. I could hear the conversation from that side of the house—not far away—wafting around to us with the smell of meat. But we were alone.

"What a view," I said.

"You've come to the right place. It's very special here. There are spirits down there in that valley. I ought to know. I've lived here all my life. You have to be here a long time—your husband will not see things as they are, believe me." Electric lights bounced up at us from houses in the valley. "If Paul's interested, by the way, I publish a magazine." He patted the peeling bark of something growing through his deck. "You like the tree? It's paperbark. I mean—I might be some help...."

We looked out at the hillside covered in eucalyptus. The air was bitter with it. We could see a man and woman talking in a house to our right, a girl brushing her hair, a child crying in another house — only a sound at first and then a light coming on and the sound fading away. "What do you mean I came to the right place?" I was still thinking of the drink, which he hadn't given me. The hillside smelled moist. As if there would be rain any minute. As if it would originate in the earth and the pungent eucalyptus leaves.

"You want this?" He handed me his beer. It seemed I could not have one of my own. The host and I, on the hilltop, huge and observant, looking down.

A pregnant woman came out to stand in the doorway, triumphant with the importance of her body.

"So — what about Paul?"

Paul didn't want another child. "Well, he does have albums and boxes of stuff at the house."

"Maybe I could come over," he suggested. I lifted his bottle.

Around the corner of the house, on the porch, someone said, "What do Canadians have to do with it?"

"Nothing. They're bombing...military...just like us.... It isn't Kahoolawe to them, it's target practice. The Hawaiians think it's sacred ground, but they can't get in....You go there, you take your life in your own hands...."

I looked at my companion. "What do they mean?"

He grinned. "Don't ask me. I'm only one small part Hawaiian. Nobody is Hawaiian any more."

"...part of the native rights movement. Restore the place.... They got a ceasefire...to do some chants...take pictures...."

My host was moving closer, humming softly, but I was listening to the unseen conversation. Paul was inside with his friends.

"Why?"

"Makes the air force or Marines or whatever look like shit."

The voices faded in and out.

"Do people here still really believe in the old religion?" I wondered out loud. "Chants and dreams?"

"Don't you?" Perhaps my question had offended him. Then he whispered in his normal, husky voice. "You can't just live the normal days of a straight wife. You find a place like this, you have to tap into its nights. Look at those photographs by your old man. He's tapping, isn't he?"

I looked down at my bare feet, at the soft cedar boards we were standing on. His feet next to mine surprised me. They were delicate and pale. His arm around my waist surprised me more. His dark skin looked soft, like cheese. But his fingers dug at my waist. There was a hole cut in the boards through which the paperbark tree grew. Under us, an abyss of dark, rocky space. "I don't think the old religion has much to do with you," he laughed, pulling his arm in, but taking mine.

I put his empty bottle down feeling mildly confused. I had been feeling that way all evening. I noticed his dark, heavy-lidded eyes and felt his warm, small hand. But Paul, as if summoned, appeared behind him, a shape in the darkness. He was edging toward us. "I'll tell Paul you're interested," I said.

With the press of his fingers still on my back I tried to sound businesslike. "How's next week? Dinner." I said.

"I'm gone then. Outer islands."

I said politely, clearly, "Well, whenever it works out for you."

"I'll consult my tide chart." He laughed. "How's the next full moon?"

I could feel Paul behind me. I swung around to see him standing there, and when he moved up beside me I leaned into him, feeling immense relief. No more mystery. No more wasted conversation. "Ready to go?" I put my head on his shoulder, comfortable again. No more party intrigue.

"There's someone from Punahou," Paul said, referring to Kit's school.

I blinked. All that was over for the year. Schedules for car pool rides. Field trips. "I couldn't. Not tonight."

"Just go talk to her. She knows a camp where Kit could go."

We were back inside. I said, "I've already said our thanks. Maybe we should head home."

"Jess, this is the best part of the party," Paul pouted, knowing already he had lost. I had done my part for art, for his career. I had even made a dinner date with a potential patron. "They're getting out guitars," he said, already backing toward the door.

I was drunk now, for sure, on wine and beer and trees. Paul was right. Someone was singing. Someone was playing in slack key and those round sentimental words—a mixture of old Hawaiian chants and Christian hymns—rose up around us, filling the room. The music followed us to the door, where Paul had trouble finding his sandals. It followed us as we wandered across the fallen flowers in the yard, where Paul had trouble again with the car keys.

"We made an appearance anyway," I said as we walked to the car, opening our separate doors and climbing in. Couples climb into cars the way they climb in bed, choosing sides.

Tonight Paul would drive home because he was moody and he couldn't add to that my choice of roads. I always take the long way down the hill, past what I'm sure was Alma's house in *From Here to Eternity*. The movie, I mean. I remember the long walk Prewitt made to her house after he killed Fatso. She loved him but the whole romance was fated from the start. For years, that movie and the picture of Revere from the magazine I had in my closet were all I knew about this place.

But Paul was in a hurry. Not for him the long curves along Alma's street, which is called Sierra Drive, for a slow transition to electric Kaimuki. He dove straight down, taking the steep descent of Wilhelmina like a fallen soul.

We plunged through the neighborhood. "Here. Hold my beer," he said. "And don't drink it. I didn't say to drink it, Jess."

"How much did you have?"

"Nice job on the deck," he said ignoring me.

"What's his name, anyway?"

"Larsen. Stealer of wives."

I was slumped back in my seat. "For half an hour of nothing, we drove all the way to town," I put in, meanly. "I'm tired. Don't forget, Paul, my time's off."

"Correct," said Paul.

Silence. We were at the bottom of the hill—the movie house, the restaurants, the stores, the oriental feel of Kaimuki. We had a favorite restaurant here, rowdy and Chinese. Since childhood I've loved Chinese food. When I was six, my aunts taught me to use chopsticks. For a while I hung paper lanterns in our house. My mother, on the other hand, while I was growing up, favored the Pennant Cafeteria in downtown Topeka. She took me there every Monday night after my ballet class. I always had the Children's Special—creamed chicken in a chicken-shaped dish. It cost a quarter and after eight weeks, eight dinners there,

I was entitled to a plastic purse. I had a collection of them in my bottom drawer.

I'd had a postcard from my mother that afternoon. Postcards were all she ever wrote. As if she thought of herself, like my father, as a traveler; maybe she wrote them in his name. "I miss you," she had scratched on the card, almost parenthetically between news of the weather and her health. I'd only been back for two days. She must have sent it before I left.

Surrounded by light now, we sped down the freeway, past Manoa, past the edge of the city, into the valley of Nuuanu, up into the mountains again. For ten years, eleven years, all our lives, we had moved closer and closer to the Pacific Ocean across that map I had described on my forearm. Now it was around us, we were surrounded by it.

I thought about Paul's shoulder in the dark, hoping he would work through his mood. I thought about his warm chest and his shoulder and my stomach up against him when we turned around to sleep. Maybe I liked the sleeping best of all—held in his curve, held against all the things that daytime did to us. Light-headed from the beer, I leaned across the space between us and patted his knee. "The house looks great," I said. "I haven't said that yet. Have I?"

My hand could feel the twitch of muscles underneath his skin. After so many years we understood each other well. The twitches and the silences. We were, I tell myself, like every husband and wife. Paul was staring out intently at the road and I was thinking about things like groceries. There weren't any eggs. There was nothing to eat for breakfast the next day. I wrote a short list in my head. The conversation we made on the drive home was desultory. It was like the party cracker I had saved for Kit and carried in my pocket, stale and crumbling.

At the house, Paul parked the car and headed for the door while I went through the dark garage to the backyard.

And as I stood there a gust of wind came up and drove some pointed mango leaves down to the ground. The sound they made was heavy, thudding, as if flesh and blood had fallen at my feet. When I walked over them, they felt like skin. I moved through the thick leaves toward the glass door and stood on the dark side of it, looking in at Paul.

He was standing, staring down at Maya stretched out sleeping on our sofa, her long arm thrown across her face like a mark of silent exclamation.

NINE

A few nights later, under a sky squeezed between trees until there was no wind, no sound at all, I lay sprawled on the grass outside our house.

There are two things to look for in a husband, Mother used to say. And when you find them, you know you've got the right man. He should make you laugh. That lasts for ever, after the other things are done. And you should want to have his children.

If we could have another child. Perfect, unmoving, like a photograph, I held our landscape in my eye, the giant Norfolk pine twinned, split by genetic impulse in its infancy into two trunks, identical, as if the sky had become mirror. This double tree had as its fall line our small house. By tipping my head back I could squash the neighborhood. I could demolish my own point of view.

The sky pressed down on me. An awful hum sang through the atmosphere — of insects, stars, and heat. The bushes with their closed and sleeping flowers touched my hair with sticky leaves and the great hum around me throbbed inside my pulse beating itself against the insides of my wrists, my heart, behind my eyes. Paul wouldn't touch me. Since I had come back he even refused me that.

If we could laugh.

I always smiled at Paul, even in argument, so that he wouldn't doubt me, wouldn't leave me. Just as my mother tended her marital flame, I tended mine. I smiled a secret sign of recognition. I smiled a sign of our connection. I smiled so there would be no wavering and no ambivalence between us.

I suppose such a night comes to everyone. Paul didn't want another child whatever else he wanted and there was no laughter between us now. But there were a few small secrets, private moments held between us like pieces of ice in all the tropical weather.

Behind me, in the house, Paul was asleep. Uncovered, he slept on our bed. For years I had felt ugly and unlovable. If my father couldn't love me, how could Paul or anyone? But finally, that night in my back yard under the mango tree, I thought, my father has not abandoned me, he's dead. Inside the house Paul slept and then he turned over slowly and reached for the bedside lamp, because one side of him, when I went back to our bedroom, was outlined in its light. It was the side away from me. Propped on a pillow he held his arms against his chest, all thwarted sleep. "What's wrong with you?"

"With me?" My throat was thickening, hands flexing, squeezing upper arms and letting go. "It's you," I said.

"So that's it," he said loudly, as if struck by my unfairness. "It's my fault!"

"Not so loud. You'll wake Kit! And the neighbors."

"You don't even know the neighbors." Paul pulled himself out of the area of light altogether so I could hardly see him, and sat up in darkness. "Anyway, I could wake the dead for all you care."

"Don't say that." I peered at him hopelessly.

"Look," said Paul knowingly. "Maybe it's time for you to quit hoping things will get better with us."

"But when did they go bad? Everything was fine before I left. Wasn't it?" I didn't want to cry. I didn't want to wake up Kit.

I have no friends here and no past, I thought miserably. I have only you, always, wherever we go.

"Look at me." I could see the gleam of his shoulder in the lamplight, in the moonlight. His skin was silvery. His muscles shivered underneath. "Look here, Jess!" Paul's face had disappeared but his voice, pillowed at first, leapt from the wall behind him, echoing, throwing itself around as if lightbeams had escaped his throat, as if his heart could be exposed. "What do you see anyway?" he demanded, choking. "Go ahead! Tell me! You don't like my values—you don't like the way I want what belongs to me. It scares you that I'm so honest, doesn't it? Really. Admit it!" he went on. "That's what's eating you. You don't even see where I belong. You don't have faith in me. Do you!"

He was furious now, suddenly beyond reach, and I trembled in the doorway. "Tell me to stop breathing. You might as well," he hissed, "tell me I'm in another world. Why don't you tell me to just get lost!"

It was Revere again. That was at the root of this, I thought. It was tormenting him.

"If that's what you want." The room widened, our small house opened up, my words were stuck in tabletops and curtains and the walls, planted around us. I tried to see us on the ancient lanai at Revere with the garden around us, with the hills on one side and the sea on the other. With the jungle behind us and the road going back to town in front. With our children moving around in the dusk on the lawn. But my words were everywhere. Importunate. "Mihana warned me," I said. I remembered the dream and the moments alone with her in her room. As if we had become too huge for the room, the objects around us looked suddenly fragile. "She's saving it all for Maya," I added. "And if she complains to even one trustee of the estate, you and Kit and I could lose everything."

"Quit stewing. I'll go join up. Then you'll get my paycheck every month."

The choice in an argument is whether to speak or not to speak, for there is no hope either way. Paul had seized the clear glass bedside lamp, while I stood frozen in our mistakes, in words, in slowed-down time, and he heaved it on a flight to open up the final secrets of the room, so that it landed smashed and rocking on its torn shade in the darkest corner, where the only light came from the moon.

TEN

When Paul put some clothes in a suitcase and backed out of the house, I didn't argue. The present had become a moving point, taking me along with it, every part of me changing so that I would not be the same person from one minute to the next. I was not the same person getting up who went to bed the night before. I was left in stunning silence, afraid for myself.

Paul, I said into the emptiness, where are you who know me? If no one's here to see me how can I know I exist? I watch my face change, losing the memory of itself. I am afraid of fading. You keep me within the limits of your reference. You keep me from slipping out of the skin boundary, from where I might fall into nothing.

I dreamed of Paul. His awful dive into an empty pool which Kit and I both saw, an act of foolishness and daring he survived and which earned her undying admiration. We put him in the car to take him home, passing all the familiar doors, one closed flat surface after another; but our own door did not appear. I wanted to fix him a meal again. But there was no place we could rest.

I woke a different person from the one who went to bed the night before. When I went through the wide doors of the living room, stepping outside to the lanai, beneath the old tin roof wrapped in green climbing plants, I sat at the glass table on a flimsy wicker chair, staring blankly at the be-still tree that chimed without a sound as if it had been hung with bells wrapped in bright yellow cloth, and at the mango tree with its green fruit.

For hours or days I lay in our wide bed, stuck to its heat and violence, stuck to the dark because our light was lying in the corner of the room. And then Mihana came. "Is she asleep?" Slamming the brakes of her pickup truck she yelled at her dogs to stay put in the back. Her voice cut through the morning as I lay in bed avoiding everything but fear.

"How many days is she holed up in all this stink?"

Four days and forty nights he had been gone.

Kit must have answered her. The front door squeaked and I could hear Mihana's slow progress through the unopened mail, the papers and laundry and cats—laundry trailed over chairs, a heap of unwashed color, papers thrown into corners and over surfaces. Kit's tape recorder in several pieces on the floor, a neighbor's cat consorting with my own.

Mihana, immense and delicate, gliding through. "You asleep in there?" The doorknob moved.

Not having slept for days or having only slept for days, I said, "No. Getting up. Come on in."

The knob twisted and she appeared in front of me, her hair wrapped up and out of sight along with all her charm and friendliness. She looked preoccupied and mean.

"You didn't come," she stated, as if I had let her down.

"To see you."

"Right. To see me."

"I've been...."

"What's this thing?" She touched the lamp with a bare toe. Its base was cracked and it was spilling sand and small shells on the floor. "So we better talk," she said. "We better talk." Remembering she'd left her bag and cigarettes behind in the truck and padding out, barefoot, to get them.

I should have got up, met her on my feet, prepared myself. But I curled up again like a sick dog and waited quietly for her to seal my fate, as if she had gone out to get that too.

"That's why I came," she said when she returned, noticing my matted hair and rooting in her bag. She never smoked at home. The bed groaned as I shifted.

She struck a match and lit the cigarette. "I didn't see them in three days," she said, exhaling, her eyes bright. "Did you?"

Whatever small defenses I'd arranged for myself vanished. I wanted her to disappear, this harbinger, this voice. But at the same moment I wanted to throw myself on her mercy and into her arms. "Them?" I cried.

"Maya and Paul."

Something let go in my back, moving around by degrees of discomfort to my stomach. I had to concentrate on that sensation which was not yet pain. Which might cause me to leave the room abruptly or to curl into a ball again. It was my only point of view and I attended to it.

"Go make some coffee. You should get up now." Mihana dropped an ash into her hand and majestically left the room.

I stood up gingerly and moved as if I'd been down with a violent disease, feeling my way to the chaotic kitchen where Mihana was balanced on a rattan stool, tough blossom huge on a wobbly stem, stubbing her cigarette out in an unwashed dish.

The day before I'd gone into Paul's room. I'd looked in the first picture box I touched. In a white holoku, Hawaiian formal dress, with flowers in her hair and *maile* covering her front, Mihana had stared up at me from the yellow box, both her arms lifted. Doing the hula, I supposed. I'd never seen her dress that way. Or dance. Had she dressed that way for him? Had he gone straight to her? Where had she seen him after he left home but at Revere? Had she harbored him?

Standing at the sink in T-shirt and underwear, resisting her, filling the kettle with warm water and rinsing the coffeepot,

I noticed first the sour, rancid smell of clutter and then her disregard for it, her complete uninterest. My body reeked of neglect and my own smell revolted me.

From the kitchen window, I looked through a plumeria tree out to the curbless street. Kit was rolling by behind the flowers on her Saturday skates. Wanting someone to play with her, to notice, she skated up and down the street in front of all the houses. It was the courting dance she performed every morning of that summer, and for a moment I was lost in admiration, watching her.

"We going to have coffee?"

I faced the stove, turned on the heat, got down two cups, and measured coffee into the drip pot. Silently I damned her, put the cups on a small tray and then remembered I hadn't put the kettle on. Paul and Maya. She must be dreaming again. But she sat there watching me, absorbed and patient, while things boiled, and I edged out of the room to get something, forgetting what it was and bumping aimlessly into things, still in my underwear and unwashed, uncombed.

When I came back to the kitchen she was waiting, smoking another cigarette while water steamed and boiled onto the burner and the stove. Remembering the awful living room, I thought of sitting with her in the ruined kitchen. That was worse. Resigned, I carried our tray to the salvaged steamer trunk that served as coffee table and offered her a chair. Small and ungracious, the setting suddenly seemed unfit for an interview, revealing my state of mind more obviously than if I'd thrown the coffeepot against the wall in front of her. Mihana settled herself on the trunk, leaving no place for the tray I was holding. I sat it on the laundry- and toy-strewn floor. Arranging herself uneasily, she leaned back and dangled her leg at me, over the edge. She looked larger each time I glanced at her.

"I wonder if it's going to help." She reached for a cup.

"What am I supposed to do?" I said. "If you think they're together."

"What you believe," she said, sipping thoughtfully, stirring some sugar in with a finger, licking it, adding some more. I had forgotten the spoons. "Listen. Maya believes in something," she said, sitting straighter on the trunk. Her eyes were fierce and dark. "And Paul believes in nothing. Or in Maya. I don't know which." Her glare threatened me with the authority of things that aren't apparent. "What about you?"

He believes in himself, I thought, like anyone, and in us and his name and this place. "Why me? You know about these things. There must be some cure out there for what ails him." I remembered the night we'd gone down to the beach at Revere, across from the islands that stood like perfect promises lapped by the water. We had gone down to the sand to sit around a fire of sticks and pine needles and charcoal, crouched around it closer and closer because of the wind that came in from the turquoise sea. We had just arrived. Everything around us was deep blue. It was the edge of the world. Infinity. We were meeting Maya and Mihana for the first time. Seeing the house. Maya was uncertain, a child still, talking to Kit as she poked at the flames. Coughing a little now and then. We didn't want her thirteen-year-old conversation though, we were drawn to her thin shoulders and small face framed by dark, wild hair. And was Mihana glad to have Paul back? Was she pleased to have us in the house? Offering things we felt entitled to—a daughter we could not know in the ordinary way? Now was that child ruined? Was my husband a beast? Even the thought of it—unbearable, ridiculous. Fix it! I felt like shouting out.

"If this is happening, it's not what you think...he's not like that...it's not anything like that. She's too young, he was annoyed at me, he's probably taken her off on some camping trip...."

I felt as oddly defensive about this child who had been so much in my care for the past year as I did about my husband. But this sympathy alternated with something uglier, the two sensations

103

riding a teeter-totter in my mind, one of them up while the other was down.

"Here there are twenty kinds of mischief with the married," Mihana announced. "An abundance, you might say. So many kinds the missionaries couldn't find enough words to translate them. They only called it 'sleeping mischief'. They couldn't find enough words. You see?"

"Which kind is this?" I said, childishly. "Make it simple for me."

"You talk like one *haole,* you." She dropped her voice, as if there were listeners, although Kit was patrolling the street. "You want one word, for all the kinds. Something to own." Her voice softened. "Something to name." I felt my eyes filling with tears.

"But I can't see...." That they were lying somewhere, shaped together, and I had to clench my teeth shut to keep them from chattering.

"What you can't see you cannot understand." Mihana stood up suddenly and lightly, pulled her purse up, and stuffed cigarettes and matches back inside. What I could see was my new loss. Mihana blaming me, expecting me to intervene, and wasn't I the injured one in this? "Sometimes I feel you in this house," I said. "As if you watch me, just like you are doing now." I hadn't felt her there before but I knew that, once she had gone, her presence would sit on the trunk like an old fetish, never budging, for as long as I lived in the house. Willing me to keep her house, her child, her island, from breaking into pieces. From all that mischief.

"Not me." Mihana frowned. "That's Kapo then. That's the old one. Madam Pele's sister. She likes *haoles* anyway. So." She turned, as if outwitted by a larger presence, and I waited for her to abandon me, wanting to call her back, to offer her my help, to form a partnership or dark conspiracy with her. But she'd never trust me now. I had ignored her warning. And there were no more dreams, or if there were she didn't tell me about them.

She was taking something from her bag. "For you," she explained. "Something I make."

"What is it?" Misty. A jar of clouds.

"For strength. I use *ilima* roots. Leaves and young shoots of *popolo*. Sugar cane. *Noni* fruit. Nothing to fear." Madame Pele is the goddess of volcanoes, I thought. What's her sister like?

I watched Mihana's delicate withdrawal from the room. Had she arrived to warn me or to heal me? To ask for help or to describe her victory?

Then I could hear the truck door slam, hear the old vehicle start up and lurch away. I stared into the hole she'd left and saw it fill up with the presence I'd expected it to have—Mihana sitting wordless, angry, disappointed, pleased. I took the jar she'd given me and twisted the lid. Roots and leaves. No smell. No flavor at all. I tasted it.

A minute or two later, I slouched down the hall.

While Kit was pursuing her reckless career on the street, I lay in the warm darkness of my bed. I thought of Maya's silly, perfect flesh. And I cried.

ELEVEN

It wasn't the usual July that year, when trade winds come in off the ocean, clearing the air, making it cool and sweet.

That summer on Oahu we had Kona weather for the worst part of July. Sticky and grim, it arrived like an uninvited traveler blown from volcanoes on the big island, its bags full of heat and sediment and gloom.

Using the heat as my excuse, I stayed inside. I sat around the house for days with this unwelcome, unexpected guest, relishing the thought that everyone beyond my walls was miserable too — that Paul and Maya, wherever they were, must be as uncomfortable as I was in the privacy of skin and bone and sweat.

Kit and I were alone together for the first time in our lives and we resented it, blaming ourselves for Paul's abandonment. I told her he had some new work for a travel magazine, and heard myself sounding like my mother. I waited for some word from him and I grew older, smaller, more afraid with every hour. Kit watched me change. She eyed me nervously, wanting attention and shrinking away at the same time.

In the heat, the swamp behind our house grew fetid and reeked of fertility. The toads and mosquitoes that lived there began to leak into the neighborhood, hopping up paved streets and flying into homes. The piles of wrecked and abandoned cars around the

Swamp Lady on her tree trunk grew to disproportionate size, and the forklift was kept busy at all hours of the day moving hunks of metal from one location along the road to another, stacking them carefully into skeletal pyramids until one vast heap threatened, at last, to shut out all sight of wild grass and stream and the old *heiau* of the early dwellers there on the hillside next to the city's garbage.

Hours and hours each day I slept, patching the ends of consciousness together and waking tired, sweaty, grim. The weather grew hotter and I was no closer to the truth. Kit begged to go to camp, even a day camp, but I could not rouse myself on her behalf. She missed her father, who would have taken her with him to the beach, who'd promised to teach her how to sail, who played with her and made her laugh.

On the hillside above the bones of cars, fires burned all day, adding thick smoke to our already crowded air. The combined effects of external heat and internal combustion made them unquenchable. Our lungs ached. Our eyes ran with tears.

The cat joined me and stretched out at my side as if he sensed that, all alone, I wandered in a nightmare place. And in my living room, Mihana waiting, watching my hot struggle patiently, unbothered by the thick air or the heat, sister to the volcano, sister to Pele, its deity. Watching me.

The street was watching for some sign from us as well, as if despair had grown as evident as weeds around the door. On Sundays, married couples came through their front doors with gloves and clippers to trim and cut efficiently while the hibiscus in my yard bore large, ferocious blossoms. Between the house and the street the fig tree dropped bitter and inedible green fruit.

Why did I see Paul on his back, apart from me, arms at his sides, chest-breathing deeply, as sincerely as a boy? This picture of him never left my mind. Where did he sleep in all that nakedness, his penis resting soft against his thigh? The soft place in his neck, just underneath the chin, filling up and emptying with each inhalation, exhalation, as if he dreamed of something lovelier than sin, as if he sailed a calm sea.

"I could go to the Y," Kit said. "They have Summer Fun."

Kailua was built in the center of an old, extinct volcano. The Koolau mountains were one side of its rim. It had sunk at some time in the past. Millions of years ago Oneawa Street had been a coral reef. Now it stretched from the Marine base to the center of town, and the bay had been filled in somehow. Another trick of Paul's ancestors, I thought, making more room for sugar cane and pineapple. The entire island was an unstable, spongy mass. Parts of it were protected and left wild so water could sink in and stabilize the water table underneath. Too much cement, too many houses and hotels, and we would all die of thirst.

As if it already belonged to someone else, I walked around the house looking at the accumulation of our lives in boxes and on walls. Paul's photographs. I began to forget that it was summer in Hawaii in 1973. I put myself into the time of each picture, the ever-present ever-past, the time of all pictures, the time without time.

In frames and flat yellow boxes we were contained. Kit in tall grass with me one summer day. Her short, bobbed hair, her yellow overalls, her bear. In this box we are good people for ever. I will always keep us this way.

I forgot the day and the hour and remembered the afternoon at Revere when I had studied the pictures on the walls. The home of a chief. A prince. A young girl. Waimea Falls. The beckoning arm of the Moana Pier, long gone. Queen Kamamalu. Queen Kapiolani. Native Flower Girls. In Hilton's home there were no family pictures; then Paul created his own legacy. And wrapped it in yellow boxes. Once I had opened an unused box by mistake and exposed fifty blank sheets. I had ruined fifty possibilities. Now the boxes were carefully marked in square letters in black ink: Family—Exposed. Kit in my lap. Kit in our bed. Paul in the grass. Paul in my heart, my head. Paul in Kansas. In California. Paul in my skin like a chigger and I take him everywhere.

And who will chop down my yellow tree?

Who will change this house, taking its rooms into another color? Who will sleep in my empty bed?

Who will trim the fig tree, causing its roots to reach into the moisture underneath the house, causing the walls to bend?

And who will eat my bread?

TWELVE

And when his absence made my heart grow fond, I thought my private thoughts until, who knows, perhaps the thinking of him caused him to come home.

"I need to talk to you," he said from a pay phone, using the word I counted on.

And I agreed. "Kit! Daddy's on his way. Quick! Get your room picked up! I need you to help. Come on. Hurry. Hurry up!"

The shells and sand in the bedroom had trickled into the hall. I had not done the laundry or emptied the trash. And there was no meat or fruit. I had not had the car. Kit had gone to the Chinese store every day, bringing us back milk and bread.

Kit was in front of the TV crumbling a piece of toast she'd spread with cinnamon and sugar. Under her crossed legs tiny crystals dribbled, calling on ants. Her lap was covered with crumbs which scattered when she stood up. "He's coming back?"

"Yes. Help me. Come on, hurry up!"

There was neglect and confusion in the house that had to be concealed and Kit and I, together, did what we could.

The dishes buried in suds, the kitchen and living room swept, I had time to brush my hair and wash my face—no match for the other woman; no match for the flawless unremarkable no-history of her face, her skin.

Kit, in her excitement, arranged papers and magazines and games incoherently. Toys went into the hall closet. Clothes were flung into the hamper in the bathroom, where I stood noticing, for the first time, that it had become a woman's place already, that in ten days all trace of Paul had vanished with his razor and comb and the red plastic bottle of aftershave.

While I checked myself doubtfully in the mirror, Paul arrived and stood at his own door, saying, "Sweetheart, sweetheart," speaking to Kit and hugging her. For a minute he did not come in, then the door squeaked open. "Oh, sweetheart"—again— "Daddy's home."

I watched their reunion from the hall and waited. He'd lost weight and had regained that crazy, crumpled look I used to love. The look he'd had when we first met, the look he'd had when we ran off together leaving my life behind. In a minute he would rush into my arms, sorrowful and apologetic, and grateful to be home.

He staggered to a chair, muttering savagely, berating himself.

"I didn't really leave you," he said, looking down into his hands as if they'd committed a crime that he had just discovered. He shook his head sadly.

He hadn't looked at me. He looked at his trembling hands until he lifted them to stroke Kit's arm.

"You did," I said coldly, coming across the room to stand by Kit. "What do you mean, you didn't! I didn't know where you were, even! Where in hell were you, anyway? And you took *our* car."

"I'm here. Don't throw it all up at me for Chrissakes! I'm here. With the car. Okay? Right now."

"So I see. Are you here to stay? Or here right now?"

He hadn't looked at me. He was engrossed in Kit and, from his crumpled position in the chair, looked at her miserably, as if she might dispense absolution.

This was no real reunion. I was not even part of it. *The* car, he had said, as if I had no claim on it. And not one mention of missing or loving us. So I snapped, "Well, you don't look especially pleased to be here! What happened? Why are you here? Who asked you back here, anyway?"

He looked up. "Don't try that," he said evenly. "I just am. Whoa! This is my house. Remember? You're my family. I live here as far as I know. I assume my clothes are still in the closet."

"Washed and ironed," I said, turning my back on him, enraged at my own ambivalence. He hadn't looked at me. He hadn't asked me to forgive him, and I went into the bedroom, waiting for him to realize his mistake, thinking of what I could have said to make it easier.

Through the thin wall I could hear Kit and Paul discussing things. She had stopped crying. She was all charm.

"Come see my new skates I got," she said, taking the lead. "They've got red stripes on the side, like this girl at school had. Carrie. Remember? Before? We got them at Holiday Mart. Where's Maya anyway? Mom said you went away on a job. Why'd Maya get to go? I wish I could go on a trip with you. Remember you were going to take me to a Checkers and Pogo show?"

I crept into the hallway again and stood quietly, where I could not be seen. But I could see the two of them. Kit slipped the skates over her bare feet and suddenly her thin straight legs were stems. The skates were flowers, angular on plastic wheels. Blossoming strangely beneath her, they seemed to be attached to her skin. She clung to Paul's arm, letting her feet slide out from under her, catching herself against him just ahead or behind her fall. A drunken dance for her father.

"Not on the mats!" I yelled from the shadows. "Take them off!"

Then for a long time he sat in the chair, drinking the beer Kit brought him—becoming obstinately drunk—and reading

113

magazines from the large pile she kept ready at his side. Timidly, I emerged from the dark hall and moved around the house, trying to appear methodical. I emptied trash into large green plastic bags and carried the bags outside to our dismal cans. What we need now is passion, I thought, picking up some fallen flowers on my way back to the house.

Inside, I put them in a shallow bowl and thought of Safeway absently. The car was back as well as Paul, who sat in the chair reading magazines like someone lost in a waiting room about to be notified of a death. Absurdly I craved the anonymous order of a supermarket—a place I could enter with a use and leave with a sense of accomplishment. A place where I'd feel like a wife again. A place where I would have things to do. I would tell Paul to wait here with our uncertainty. And when I came back we'd begin again.

But if I go, he'll leave, I thought. He'll slip away. He hasn't said a word to me yet. I want him to do that, at least. Apologize. I want him to explain himself to me.

But Paul went into Kit's room then, a visitor from someplace else. And I got out ten days' worth of ironing and sprinkled water on it. I soaked beans for a pot of soup. This work is comforting, I thought. I don't know how to speak to him, how even to begin to ask him what he's done to Mihana's child and Kit's best friend. And these tasks require order. I comprehend, in this blouse and this shirt and this dress, the week before and week after. Here the days fall neatly into place and hangers fill with prospects. Beans soften and expand predictably.

A brief rain began to come down between the leaves, falling against soft surfaces and beating against the roof and street. The sound of it had the effect of separating us from everything else, from everyone, the way it curtained us when we lay in our bed under the mango tree. The rain of Mihana's old god Lono, who promised to come back. Paul was back, at least, and inside the safety of our house. The dinner had to count. One of us, I told myself, had to save this family.

At five o'clock, I trembled hopefully as we sat down to it—three people hunched embarrassed over soup bowls, Paul saying nothing. Three spoons scraped against three bowls, holding their own conversation, and Kit's made a small clicking sound against her teeth. Handed down from Paul's grandmother, the bowls had always reassured me. I'd set the table with our best.

What could we talk about? Kit wouldn't say a word and I tried to fill in the gaps by offering the salt or asking for a piece of bread. Between the words, we heard each other swallowing.

"You put that Chinese parsley in the salad?" Paul asked, finally.

"Yuck," said Kit.

"Just a hair."

"I think I got the whole hair." He pushed his chair back and stood up, wiping his hands across his jeans and catching his own look in the dark reflection of the room's glass doors. The rain had stopped and the smell from outside was clean and inviting, like a pear that had been cut open and left ready. Perhaps the weather would break at last; the evening would grow cool. We would forgive each other's trespasses. Meanwhile Paul stretched, watching himself in the doors, and sighed sadly. Then he went to our room.

When had I washed the sheets? Or made the bed?

Kit and I finished our soup and cleared the table. I left the dishes in the sink. "Go get Daddy to read to you," I said. I thought, while I take a bath you must redeem this meal, child. While I take a bath you've got to make the subtle claim of family bond. A bath, and I'll be fine again. A bath, and then I'm clean.

Running it, shattering the silence with the battle cry of water, and adding perfume, I wondered if Paul felt alliance to my flesh at all after the furtive journeys through it in the years behind us. But there was the fact of it between us. In all the words and acts

115

of love, written right in our skins, there was alliance, some shared claim. If nothing else, there was our child. There was complicity. And after that there was the child we might still have. The one we hadn't had. And blame.

Climbing into the water's heat, I lay back and studied the shower curtain, with its film of mildew. If I listened hard, around the sounds of dogs and cars and neighborhood TVs there was the sucking of the tide. The beach was wide and flat near our house. There was no crashing surf, only the labored breath, in out, in out, of an ancient beast. I would put on the green silk kimono and float in to him, relaxed and clean. I would put on the green silk kimono, the past behind us, yielding. I shaved my legs and cupped water into my body with my hand. I sat in a tiny tub of water on the edge of an unfamiliar place. I scrubbed my feet. I went barefoot so much of the time that they were stained by the red Hawaiian earth.

I would seduce him, as I had in school. In perfume and the silk kimono and the earrings he had given me when we eloped, I would come out of the bathroom as softly as I had crept into his bed when we made soft and silent love for the first time. The night things changed for me because my body changed. I was in awe of him. I lay against him, I put his hands between mine, pushed his body down with mine until where was he and where was I, where were my limits? I was disappearing in my flesh. And did he call out to me? Hope I would notice his cry? I was beyond calling. I didn't think about my choices after that night. Things were decided, after that, for me.

In the same way, when Kit was born and I saw the wreck of myself under the hospital sheet, scarred and flattened, I asked the nurse to pierce my ears so I could finally wear the gold hoops Paul had given me. The thought of putting holes in my body had seemed unnatural but after Kit's birth, my act of reproduction done, like a spider I resigned myself to mortality and its flaws.

Now, even with the pleasant image of bikini left like a negative there, I still felt hopeless as I looked at my body.

In perfume and the green kimono and the earrings, I came out of the steamy bathroom to say goodnight to Kit and to find Paul. The streets had dried off and the grass was full of soggy blossoms, pink and white and yellow, that had been washed from the branches of trees. The air smelled full and wet, and doors up and down the street were opened wide. No doubt the neighbors had noticed the car and drawn conclusions.

Around us, pulled closer by the darkness, the houses had the glow of lamps and television sets. The sounds of the programs occasionally intruded, loud and self-mocking, often in pidgin, especially the news and the ads which were larded with swimming pools, barbecues, surfers, and bikinis. But our house was quiet. Except for Kit's small light, the house was dark, as if we needed nothing.

Kit was lying on her bed, arms at her sides, eyes staring up at me. I opened her arms and kissed her soberly, suspended over her desire, her thoughts. "Nighty-night," I whispered, turning the light out, and patting dark air for a moment in the hall.

In our room, Paul was stretched out on the bed, sleep-breathing his reproach. The bedside lamp was unrepaired. The arid smell of failure was in the room. It was too large to cross and I was large and ugly and absurd in my kimono, my hair stiff. My belly had been puckered by a hundred pregnancies. I heard an insect clicking on the wall close to Paul's face.

I wanted to walk over and reach out and touch his shoulder then, to wake him and, in the darkness, to stretch out next to him.

But I couldn't move. I stood there stunned, addressing him silently in the great silence that engulfed us. And underneath, the fig tree pushed toward us its tentacle-like roots, tilting the poured-cement foundation and the walls. I stood there silently and watched him sleep, seeing his wallet on the chair next to his watch. With a long reach, I lifted it and looked inside.

Money. There wasn't much left in the bank. Paul had emptied our account. But I didn't count what he had. He had come home. I wanted him to ask me to our bed. His body was breathing rhythmically as if it couldn't be disturbed, as if the space around him were untouchable. Inside the wallet there was a white pill. I took it out and placed it on my tongue and put the wallet back.

My family asleep, Valium whizzing between heart and stomach, I walked to the living room. At least he's here, I thought, satisfied that the other one was more alone than I was, the terrible almost-woman child. He isn't in her arms, he's home, he's in our bed and we'll straighten things out tomorrow, I thought, pulling the silk around me. After we talk it out, after he explains things and asks forgiveness and asks me to take him back. Somewhere a silver gecko clicked and from the beach a breeze blew in. I heard the wall clock tick, the new fridge buzz, sounds I was unused to at night. As if the house around us were alive. Safe in my privacy, tall and unbeautiful in the green kimono, I slept in the living room, alone. And before dawn, as I lay on the sofa wrapped in the silk cocoon of my middle life, there were sounds in the study—hands ruffling paper and stacking things. Paul was on the floor with drawers and boxes spread around him. From under his door a dim light was leaking out.

In the kimono, I advanced, knocking very gently, asking him if he'd like a cup of coffee.

"I'd like to talk," he said, moving a box aside to pull the door open, then looking up. The uncombed hair and unshaved face gave him the look of someone who'd lost touch with normal conversation. But I went in to him. It dawned on me, for the first time, that he was afraid. Maybe I looked the same.

"I thought you'd wait up for me," I admitted, towering over the chaos around him.

"Sit down," he said, awarding me the only chair. "Look. Yesterday. I'm sorry." He waved an apologetic hand. "The problem...is...well, I guess I need time.... I...."

"With her," I said tightly. "A fourteen-year-old girl." Daylight was just visible now, through the dirty louvers of his room. The objects on the bookshelves and desk began to stretch in the filtered light. The island, porous as sponge, was opening.

"...to get organized," he finished.

"Organized? I'd like to know what it is you are doing that has anything to do with organized."

"How would you.... It isn't what you think!" he said in a loud whisper. We were speaking softly out of habit, so that Kit wouldn't hear. We were breathing in the air that the island exhaled from its flowers and vines and dense undergrowth. All that oxygen. "Just for a while," he said, as if I could grant absolution. "I have to be on my own." Accusing me of selfishness. His earnest eyes searched mine.

"Fine," I lied acidly.

"Just for a while," he said again. He added feebly, "I can't seem to get hold of myself."

Sitting at his desk, in the uncomfortable straight-backed chair, I had an impulse to stand up and throw it clear across the room. Always, between us, his helplessness was his defense. Instead I cried, "Have you lost your mind? And with Kit's friend! A baby! Oh God, Paul. Not to mention she's Mihana's daughter. You're throwing away everything! It can't be Maya you want! She's a child! It must be that godforsaken house!"

He laughed. A kind of croak. "Tell me about it...."

"Kit thinks you came back," I countered, from the hard chair. "Why'd you let her think that if...."

"I'm leaving."

"No."

"Before she's out of bed." He stood up. "You can keep the car."

"Good. Fine. Run away again. But don't forget that what goes on between you and Maya goes on here, too. I'm part of it. Kit's part of it. I'll make sure Kit knows just exactly what goes on with both of you! What's Maya?—a child—an innocent. I can't believe you'd.... What can she know about...anything? All the years and intentions and what's between us!" I was trembling, my jaw ached, I could hardly keep myself from holding him back, shutting the door so he couldn't leave, so he wouldn't ruin our happiness. But Paul was impatient. He couldn't wait.

Stiffly, he bent over to shove what was close to him on the floor into a cardboard box. He gathered everything in range. "So I go," he said foolishly, adding a final stack of papers to the box and lifting it, fat child on his hip, ready to leave.

For a moment, we were squeezed together in the doorway of the study. I stepped back. With his box, Paul stumbled into the hall and crept past Kit's room.

"Tell her...." He paused and adjusted the box as I followed him into the living room. "Tell her I'll be seeing her," he promised, balancing the weight of his responsibilities more carefully against his hip.

Then, kicking the screen door open with his foot, he pushed it out against the morning.

"Why did you change the house?" I called.

Endless Saturday had finally begun.

THIRTEEN

Kit and I kept our separate counsels. Everything in the house seemed to tick tick tick. There was the television. The cat. There was the yard which held its promises and I wandered nervously under the tree, the bush, the sky. It was a small yard with a fence of narrow laths. I went in circles, around and around. I looked at the tree I'd planted, which was taller, already huge and covered with those silent yellow bells that shook soundlessly in the humid air. That weekend I wrote a letter to my mother, telling her that we were fine.

The morning leaked away; and the day turned into something hot, impatient, fragile with woe. There was the house, there was Revere, Maya would inherit it, Paul would live there with her. They would sit together on the long lanai looking out over the immense garden, through the jungle, down to the sea. He and his native child-bride.

He used to say it's women who calculate. While men go at life straight from the gut, women are thinking, thinking, figuring.

In one or two respects he may have been right. For one thing, there's the body. There are the scars we wear. They represent things earned, they are like photographs. Each scar tells of a real event. Wear is another thing. To watch as your own face assumes the look of someone's unforgiving dog speaks of a life lost. Waiting and worrying. The calculation has to do with how we use our scars, how we offer them up for scrutiny as carefully as any stripper peels away the fan and the long gloves. Paul knew that between men and women claim was at the heart of everything. And scars. He knew they were my claim on him.

FOURTEEN

And now the shape of a stranger in my living room. The stiff defense of words. The ticking clock. His hands, which stayed inside his pockets.

"I forgot." When I spoke, I sounded worn.

He looked amused. "Me or the full moon? I did say I'd be here."

"I thought Paul would be here. He's away. You've caught me off guard."

"Well, I'll be on guard, don't you worry. For both of us. So why don't you feed me and I'll keep you company? I brought the wine."

Since he didn't produce it, I gave him a beer, feeling a Midwestern sense of responsibility for him now that he was in my house. For a while I tried to discuss his work at the gallery, then I tried to discuss local politics until my ignorance became obvious. I couldn't take him into Paul's room to see the photographs. There was nothing there.

At five-thirty I started cooking our dinner. There was not much to offer. Shrimp from the freezer. Rice. Cooking for company has always been a test that requires my fullest concentration. I seize up. And the more important the test, the more likely I am to rush through the preparations and spill or burn or undercook the food.

From the living room my guest, who had still never been properly introduced, shouted, "Anything I can do?"

I shouted back, "Did you say you brought wine? Do you want to put it in the fridge? Should you bring it in? Is Larsen your first or last name?"

"It's out in the car."

Had the length of his stay been in question? I heard him stand up and start for the door and I studied the curled gray shrimps in front of me. I thought how unpleasant the evening was going to be, maintaining this half-pretense of flirtation, and I thought about Paul and Maya. Not at Revere — or would Mihana, maybe, let them in? We were better friends than that...unless she did it to keep track of them. This man—Larsen—must know everything. By now, everyone we'd ever met here must know the whole situation. I peeled the shrimp angrily—all of them, all of them knowing it all. I wrapped the peels in newspaper and washed the rice, imagining Maya sliding down the long hall of Revere carrying her pure heart in her hands like a tray of food—pale shrimp, white rice, clear sauce, Paul waiting for her in his father's study by the sea, unpacking a cardboard box and reading titles on the spines of books, making enough space on the shelves for his own things.

My guest came in with his warm wine and narrowly missed colliding with Kit who was moving, skates in hand, toward the door. He leaned against the kitchen wall as if his presence would appease me.

"So where's the old man?"

"He's doing...some background work...on his family place...."

"Ahh, over in Lanikai, right? I've seen it from a distance. Spectacular. It's still a private home.... You guys have a piece of it?"

I brought the rice to a boil, a great cloud of steam gathering over the stove. Get out the condiments, I thought. Wash lettuce and let drain on paper towels. More beer. My mother uses newspapers. She swears that newspapers are clean. That's why they're used during home births. All of our salads steeped in printers' ink. Cat hair and crumbs all over the damned table. He may be finicky. Get down the plates. Tell something. Any anecdote. Smile at him. Stand here and talk.

"So when will he be back?" Measuring my obvious distress.

He had washed in like a drifter, the bearer of new scars.

"I'm not sure. He's around."

"But there is plenty here for me to look at. Isn't there? He doesn't care what I sell as long as I sell, does he?"

The sauce was ready sooner than I expected, its clotted, uneven colour reminding me to finish up the salad and call Kit to get an extra chair and get the table set.

She had someone in hand, one of the kids from the house next door, who looked as surly and bad-tempered as I felt. Without Paul and Maya to play with, she was as desperate for company as I was.

"Two chairs," I said. "And knives and forks."

The four of us sat down. "Let's get the wine anyway," Larsen remembered. Kit watched him and pushed her food around.

"Tell him what happened at the beach," I prompted her.

"What is this anyway?" said the neighbor child, looking at her plate.

"The fake leg?" Kit wondered.

"That's it."

"Yucky!" said the neighbor child as I served up the rice. "Anyway, where's your dad?"

Neatly, she folded back the curry sauce as if she were unveiling something useful and important, and proceeded to eat every grain of rice, leaving the sauce.

"I told you," Kit said, tossing her hair back and carefully avoiding me. "He's traveling around taking some photographs. He's a photographer. You can see his pictures everywhere all

125

over this house." She did not indicate them by any gesture but spoke as if this kind of professional biography would be known and accepted by everyone else on the block.

"He's on assignment," I added. "You want some more?" I asked the neighbor child. "Kit, get her some more."

Kit threw me a despairing look. "I thought you wanted me to tell the story," she said in an unpleasant voice.

"I do. Go on. I'll get the rice myself." I shuffled out and Kit told both of them, with her head down and her words falling into her plate, about a man who'd asked her to watch his things while he went swimming, then left everything on his towel including his artificial leg.

"I thought he was just going to leave maybe sunglasses and stuff. And he had to hop and I was stuck!" She laughed loudly. "It was horrible! Was it ever horrible!" No one seemed to be listening. Kit's lip was twitching. I thought she was suddenly going to cry. Instead, she dropped her spoon on her white plate.

"Why don't you two go on and play," I suggested, because she was looking vague and blotchy.

Relieved at their departure, Larsen pushed his chair back and looked across at me. His hands were gripping his belt and I saw him aligned against me too — Paul and Maya and Mihana, and him. Even Kit. "Look, I'm not here to interfere," he said. But here you are, strange bird in my nest, I thought, reminding myself of his age and his unattractive teeth. "I'll clear the table," I said, reminding him that I was without allies, that I was alone, that I needed kindness.

I stared past him, out through the screen door and across the street, where a dog was chewing something in a yard. The air had given up its tight grip on the heat and was soft now, and ripe-smelling. His unfamiliar hands were still tight on his belt. "I wish I could help."

"With the dishes?" I thought he might put his arms around me. I was smiling at him, tasting the thin beginnings of hypocrisy in my mouth.

He seemed surprised. "I—" he began. And then a yell from Kit's room interrupted us and we both jumped. How dare you! I thought, charging down the hall. Kit slammed her door and the neighbor child brushed past me in the narrow space between the thin, reverberating walls. There is no insulation in Hawaiian houses—the smallest fracas and they fall apart.

I flicked a light on. "What's the matter here? Kit! Let me in!"

Kit was in tears. "Shut up, shut up, shut up," she cried, behind her door.

"Kit! Let me in!"

Silence.

"Come on...."

Nothing.

"Open up!" I shouted, shaking the doorknob until it gave suddenly in my hand, and I faced my daughter's look, her condemnation.

"Don't act like that," I said between teeth clenched like fists. Kit's stare was humbling. At moments when I least could stand surveillance, she was there, seeing things that weren't meant to be seen. "What did you do to her?" I demanded, standing in her doorway, at the middle of the house, attacked from all sides. "What did you do!"

"Mom, get him out of here!" Kit managed to say almost without opening her lips, but my eyes narrowed and she stared back at me until I kicked the door back, and, huge and terrible, grabbed at her shoulders, shaking them, skeletal under my hand, Kit fleeing to the bathroom, slamming the door. I remembered suddenly the only time I'd ever hit Paul, standing in the same spot by the bathroom door. I'd held back my complaints or my argument, as usual I'd smiled through whatever disagreement we were having, I'd kept myself aloof. But this time it was enough to unleash Paul and he'd lunged at me wildly with a fist that went into my arm. Instead of crying, I'd swung my own fist into his eye, knowing for the first time the energy of violence to bone and skin. I had been buoyant, cleaned of my anger, washed of the argument I had held back, and I realized I'd come into a precious commodity, a thing that put you beyond conscience, like passion or jealousy or revenge.

I turned back to the room where Larsen sat, head nested on his folded arms like an unwanted, unhatched egg. Despondency on my account? It seemed unlikely. The clock ticked soberly as I waded over and crouched beside him.

That night I felt more out of place than anyone in paradise. Larsen belonged here. Like Maya. If Paul could belong, so could I.

"Is she hiding out in there? You have any ice cream in the house?"

I gazed up, looking from below at Larsen's face. His teeth, forming those words, were out of place here, trying to be kind. Paul's teeth familiar bones watched talking, chewing, biting, bumped up against without a foreign taste. Bare bones. And now Larsen being kind. I wanted to wake up having been held by someone, to join Paul in this adventure of infidelity. And make it possible for him to come back to me. I wanted to inflict hurt, so he would have to come back to me. I nodded at Larsen. He jerked up and went toward the bathroom door, retrieving Kit.

As I pointed them toward the new fridge, Larsen and I exchanged looks. With Kit, I exchanged looks and positions. I retired to the bathroom she had vacated and locked the door. In the linen cupboard, tucked behind a stack of faded towels, I found my diaphragm, unused for weeks, unloved, and sniffed at it. I turned the faucet on and washed it off, then sniffed again. The tube of gel. Squatting awkwardly on the chipped linoleum, I squeezed

the gel onto the diaphragm, then pinched the rubber thing between my fingers and pushed it up into myself, uncomfortable at
first, a barrier between my body and the world. Then I unlocked
the door and opened it and went to Kit's room to give her a brief,
maternal kiss, all sins forgotten. She sat in an unhappy compro-
mise over the bowl of ice cream, knowing its price had been her
rage, that normally she was forbidden to take food into her room.

Larsen was sitting again, over the uncleared plates and the cold
food. "Asleep?" he queried, as if once out of his sight Kit might
cease to exist. "Let me just put these dishes...."

"No," I said, reaching out sadly then, to take his arm, changing
its course and redirecting it. He took my other hand, squeezing
it hard. I felt each finger pressing individually against the flesh,
as they had earlier against the belt, and for a moment I leaned
against him with closed eyes, smelling his hair and clothes,
feeling his damp T-shirt under my hand. T-shirts with cryptic
messages and sneakers were apparently his uniform, but he was
too old to look young in them. Worse the dull brown shoes he had
worn tonight. The point of one of them peered from the corner
of the sofa, unconnected, missing its dull mate.

Outside, the moon on its hunched back cradled the blank night
sky. The trees were pewter. Across the street the dog still chewed
on something dismal and discarded in its yard. Someone in a
house behind us was listening to the radio. Someone was playing
mah-jongg. Ivory tiles cracked meaningfully, voices were raised.

Larsen was leaning forward. He squeezed my thigh. A futile
claustrophobia moved through the room. At length I simply took
him by the hand. Into the unused bedroom. Toward my unused
bed. The room appeared to be the wreck of a past life, its mess
exposing me for an abandoned wife. We stood, up to our ankles in
this muck, and waded through it stubbornly, pushing everything,
even the old lamp, out of the way. Larsen pulled his T-shirt off
as if the disappointments of the evening had collected there. Its
surfing emblem curled at his feet. He scratched his arm absently

and, perhaps wondering what he should say, ran his own fingers through his black and white hair.

Oddly, although I hadn't really thought of her in days, my mother's face appeared. She was smoking a cigarette. She only smokes in bed. Therefore, although I couldn't see her fully, she must have been stretched out the way she always was in the carved frame of her walnut bed, waiting for me to give my latest report. Perhaps the time had come to tell Mother the truth. But I'd lost the habit. Because of my ability to cause her pain, I'd learned early to dissemble. When I was old enough to follow other girls to dances, I came home telling her that I'd had the most fantastic time, that everyone had admired the shoes or dress she had chosen for me. In truth, if someone had admired or desired me, it would have been her pleasure that I felt, not my own.

Mother, I said, you were right about that touch of coriander in the curry sauce. Of course he loved it and stayed on afterward, he was enchanted with the house, my clothes.... I slid my skirt off and Larsen turned toward me and closed his eyes as if he wanted to protect us both.

Glad that his eyes were closed, I pressed against him, smelling his skin as if he had been sent to me to claim, as if I might have to recognize him in the dark some night and call out his identity. "What's my name?"

"Jess," he said.

I drew back to see if he'd opened his eyes. "What is it?" I whispered, moving my fingers slightly, to encourage him. In the dark room his skin reflected the amber street lights which filtered in through the dense mass of mango leaves outside and made him look like a dappled animal. His hair was the coal-black and white of a middle-aged Asian man. He unfastened his belt and in a minute stood in my bedroom in his white cotton underwear.

I wanted to hurt Paul in his adventure. I wanted to be guilty too, so he wouldn't be afraid of me.

But Larsen opened his eyes and we stood still, examining the bed. Its accumulated miseries, its bits of rice and bread, its magazines and wadded Kleenexes. The wreck of it ended all hope.

"It's a small island," Larsen said thoughtfully. He kicked at his shirt. "What time does the kid get up?"

Kit become alien child, judged by this man whose jeans I'd never washed, whose hair I'd never picked out of the bathtub. "Early," I said.

He turned his feet around on the matted floor and stood there stiffly, stretching, pushing his arms into the air. I watched him dress—jeans, T-shirt pulled from the floor, slipped on again. Not the fine morning dance of my husband. The shape of my room had been invaded by a foreign guest, a person whose belongings were familiar to other rooms and other women, no part of me. Nothing is part of me, I thought. And once he'd put his jeans on there wasn't any trace of him left in the room. I brushed a few stray hairs from the humid sheet and ran my hand along the imprint of my husband on the bed.

My guest put his wine glass on the bedside table, a gesture, not quite abandonment, for my own good. Later I'd wash it out and throw it in the trash, under the kitchen sink.

FIFTEEN

Kit wouldn't talk to me. She turned away when I approached. She stayed in her room or outside all day, passing me on her skates.

"Mom, I could still get into Summer Fun," she pouted. But I couldn't give her up, I needed her to fill my day. Instead, I sent her to the beach, I cooked her favorite meals — cornbread, spaghetti, and baked ham—and she slumped over her food, letting it grow cold on her plate.

I couldn't sleep. My sleep was scattered by the dreams, the undertow of fear that pulled me cold into the dark. I couldn't swim myself back out of it. The boat disappearing. The camera. Paul. I'd get up, walk around the darkened hours, the dreams still in my mind, Kit crying an infant cry, Mihana poised like a carved figure in the air, and with her the questions, where is your husband? Where has he gone with my child? There was an answer too, but the words were all tangled and unreadable and I couldn't see them in the crowded air.

I needed help. But the answer didn't only concern Paul, it concerned Maya too. I thought Mihana might be the only hope I had.

It must have been then that I turned away from my own values and my own past. Perhaps Mihana had no wisdom, no older truth, but she seemed to understand the things that happen between people. Perhaps she understood something about Paul that I couldn't even see.

I found her by the long, pale, gravelled drive where she was gardening, wearing her large lauhala hat. Her muumuu fell in folds around her like a curtain, and into its pockets she was tucking pieces of an oversized aloe. She used it for a foul-tasting stomach medicine.

The succulents had overrun a bed of Julia's rare plants. As usual, Mihana was letting nature take its course.

I got out of the car, slammed the door, and stood behind her, but she pretended not to hear. She was singing something to herself, softly.... *"He kahuna hai e, ka u la lanoai...ka awa a Lono ma...."*

"I don't see what you're up to," she announced suddenly, spinning around. "What you have in mind! You scaring Paul away like that. So where is Maya now? What do you have in mind?"

She moved toward me, pulled some pruning shears out of a pocket, and snapped ferociously at a plant.

I said, "Me! What was that song about? You call her back. You had the warning."

Mihana laughed, creasing her sun-hardened face. "Oh you Jess! You think I'm standing here in this hot bed of cactus doing some trick?" She dropped her arms and put her head back and laughed some more. I said nothing. I stood there, looking at her. "The warning—you didn't listen anyhow. And that song was for Lono."

"And you still pray to him. Will that help Maya? What's Lono do in return?"

"Just that. Returns. He comes back. He has his time. Then he goes away. If not he gets sacrificed. So? I can still sing." She took her hat off and shook out her hair. "It's hot. I'll take you in...."

"I dreamed I saw him dive into an empty pool," I told Mihana, thinking it might be the bait she'd need.

She ignored that. "Maya wants to feed him, she wants to live with him."

I said, "There is this house. It could be his." But I was wrong, of course, they would all live here like a tribe. Now I have my family, had been Mihana's words. "I know how he feels about this house. If you had given it up, he would have left Maya alone."

"Stop daydreaming!" Mihana ordered. "Think what you ask of me."

We had moved from the garden into that dark hall, followed, once more, by the dogs, and into the small sitting room where I saw whatever flowers she had taken earlier, planted at lazy angles in a bowl. The bamboo blinds around the room were half-closed against glare. I edged into a chair across from her.

"You know about the old plants," I began quickly. "You offer cures. I'm asking for your help. You must know other things. Maybe he would give up Maya if he knew why he lost this place."

"And so you come to talk to me about cures. I know little. Very little. The garden was planted with many things even before I came. You know." I didn't. She was mysterious about her age and secretive about her past.

"You know how to fix some things...."

"Like your marriage?" she laughed hoarsely. But her face clouded. "What you say for the hula master—you know—when you want to learn, you say 'Let me in, I'm cold.' "

"Hula?"

"And that teacher answers this, 'All I have to offer is my voice.' "

"He will have all this if he ever marries her," I pointed out again, waving my hand around. "Are you going to give in to him?"

Mihana closed her eyes.

"Also, if you let Paul move in, what will it do to Maya? Think of that."

Mihana leaned back as if she had expected me, had known that I would come, and couldn't bother now with tea or courtesy. Her hands covered her knees, and she rocked gently forward toward the table and backward against the sofa as if she heard an instrument somewhere behind us.

I looked around the room. Everything futile, hopeless, stupid. I'd stepped into a hall of mirrors.

Mihana stood up. She was offering me no answers or solutions, that was obvious. When I looked up she stood close to me, her hat still on, her face beautiful. Her voice was kind.

"You go upstairs. Lie down. I'll bring you some tea."

Upstairs I wandered toward Mihana's bed and past her desk. I walked around the room and bent to look out at the waves. If Paul could have this place he'd give up Maya — or, failing that, if Mihana said she'd take it away from both of them if they were together, he might come home. In Lanikai the sea is audible, urging the sand to come away, to quit the place. Where there was once a flat white strip of powdery beach, there is now nothing at all. Green lawns and gardens drop abruptly into waves. "But I don't hear anything." I said it aloud, my voice sounded a little frightened even to myself. I missed the sight and sound of Paul's boat, the rigging hitting the mast. There was an old worn booklet on top of a pile of things there, and I ran my hand over its cover— hand-sewn, made of paper, frayed and brown, like skin that had been burned and healed. It had the look of something intimate, the look of something fashioned by a woman, and I opened it and touched a brittle page. "GARDEN ENTRIES" it said on the inside front cover, printed carefully, and underneath, in a firm hand, were three initials. JNQ. Julia Needham Quill. It was Paul's mother's then, a record of her gardening. I turned a page and then another. There were some articles pasted in. A recipe for plant food for "varieties that bloom" and, in between these and some notes and diagrams, personal entries written in by hand. They spanned the years 1937, when Julia was married, to 1941, when Paul was three. She had died during the war. Paul always seemed to forget exactly when. I glanced at a page: *I am certainly too old for another child.* And another one: *Apparently the child is to arrive tomorrow after all....*

I took the booklet off Mihana's desk and slipped it in the waistband of my skirt. I stood up and waited then, standing very straight because I was afraid to bend the fragile book. It was Paul's mother's, after all. Mihana might have lent it to me if I'd asked, but it was Paul's mother's diary. I thought I had a right to borrow it.

"I give you a small gift," Mihana warned me from the stairs. I heard her climbing them and stood listening to her approach.

She held out a fist. In it a fist-sized stone wrapped in a leaf.

"You're giving this to me?" I asked, as if we were discussing vegetables or recipes.

"An offering," was what she said. In her other hand she held a glass of tea.

I looked at her.

"If you go to the *heiau*," she explained. She was panting from the exertion of the stairs. "This is what you leave there."

Apparently I'd wasted my hope on her. She knew why I'd come but all she offered me were puzzles and charades.

"You'll need something to drink," she said quietly, as if preparing me for a journey.

SIXTEEN

On the way home, I pulled the car over to the side of the road a few feet above the boat ramp. I was reluctant to go back, thinking that while I was gone Kit might emerge from her room and eat the food I'd put out on a plate for her. The perfect islands were behind me, emerging from the water like two green knees, one more bent than the other, hung with thin circles of beaches. No one ever went to the islands. They appear, to this day, to be untouched, as if they are tabu, silently dangerous. They are farther away than they look, miniatures of their larger sister. Ahead of me, at the end of the bay, was the Mokapu Peninsula, where the Marines had their base. It must have been the first thing the Polynesian settlers saw as they approached from the Marquesas on their enormous double-hulled canoes. They must have seen the edge of the sunken crater and the huge shallow bay, now filled in, where our house sits. It would have extended all the way to the marsh, where they anchored for the first time, where they began gathering stones for a temple so they could worship their own god. The marsh—or swamp—was a large lagoon, with that coral reef that is Oneawa Street protecting their first settlement from tides and storms. Lights were beginning to come on along the shoreline where it circled Kailua Bay, and above them the stark hill that gave the Marine base its authority loomed black and stiff. The notebook had been pressed against my skin, and it was damp. Now I reached under my shirt, hunched my back, and brought it out. Small bits of yellowed paper crumbled in my hand.

Paul's mother had been an amateur botanist, respected in her day. Looking through her beginning text, with its array of notes and Latin names and planting dates, I could for the first time put a shape to her garden that appeared so wild now.

The beginning pages were given over to newspaper articles about the wedding—a private ceremony in the garden at Revere. 1937. There was a notice about the start-up of the Windward Botanical Society, the organization that had ultimately received, in fact, the major portion of Hilton's wealth. There was a newspaper clipping with a picture of Amelia Earhart attending a party in her honor in Waikiki. She was wearing a coconut-fiber hat and leis up to her ears. She was smiling broadly—standing by two people who might be Hilton and Julia. The entry read:

Last night such excitement. We entertained the famous Miss Earhart, Aka surpassing herself with an array of dishes. Mr. Vesey began to talk about sugar and conditions in the fields. What will happen if there is war. A heated discussion ensued, Hilton taking a strong position about social welfare and the preservation of native customs, but I listened, instead, to A.E.'s description of attire for the woman aviator (aviatrix?): a sports costume and close-fitting hat, low heels (the backs get scuffed while working the pedals). The problem of sunburn. She carries cold cream in the cockpit. Mrs. V. discussed an experimental clearing of the "uluhi" fern (which has invaded native forests and prevents reproduction).

It was undated. The following page had a note at the top. It read:

March 18, 1937, Hilton's 48th Birthday. A curious conversation with Miss Earhart, who, when I asked her what she missed most during her visit to the islands, insisted, "Flowers!" But I pointed up. I said, look, they are all overhead in the trees. Here they are not set out in beds.

March 20. Horrible luck. Nothing is being said but the plane with Miss Earhart and Mr. Mantz and Noonan had trouble. It "ground looped" as she was heading down the runway on Ford Island and skidded to a halt on its belly. Fortunately the gasoline tanks didn't explode. Not too serious except for publicity. This was only the 2nd leg of a round-the-world flight!

I turned the pages, finding most of the entries dated.

Jan. 2, 1938. Quarterly meeting last night of the Society, with Ray Jerome Baker illustrating use of motion pictures for biological records. (He's a photographer not a biologist.) His camera shows movement that is not apparent to the naked eye. Condenses time. The scenes showed spider lily, hibiscus, cup of gold, termites, and mosquito larvae.

March 5. Natural selection does not explain the pure adornment of a plant: patterns which cannot be useful to attract or repel.

March 16. It seems I'm going to be a mother.

April 15. Mrs. V. is declining. Yesterday talked about a boat trip, the other shore, squeezing my hand. Today it was the native race on her mind again, and she is impressed with its decadence. The lehua blooms to cheer me. They call it Madam Pele's flower. I'm not, according to Mrs. Luahi, supposed to pick it unless I make the Madam an offering, or we will have rain. Likely because, other than at Revere where it is propagated, it grows in rainy zones. But I don't hurt her feelings by saying this.

I touched the pages cautiously, still warm and damp from my own skin, from my belly, as if I had produced them myself unconsciously. I was sweating. The weather, hot again, was about to change.

May 2. Mrs. V. has taken a turn. We are left with prayer.

May 5. Put in hibiscus from a cutting from Princess Kaiulani's home which has now gone to subdivision. Grass huts were still scattered along the beach and through the groves the last time I saw it and took my cutting. Peacocks stepped elegantly through the planted birds of paradise. The stream running through Waikiki was full of ducks. Now I have to close my eyes to see the old Waikiki. The place of chiefs and royal residences is almost buried under the Moana and the Royal Hotel.

May 10. Attended benefit for the Society: latest fashion in bathing "ensembles". They were silly. I won't be wearing anything like them for a while.

May 15. I am in charge of a spray of crotons for Mrs. V.'s memorial service. Seems an odd choice for the Society to outside eyes, but that is our board for you. She was a specialist.

She must have put the book down for over a year. Maybe during that time, at least for a while, she was holding Paul. It resumed after some empty pages.

June 2, 1939. Mr. Yoshida, my new gardener, says our problem must be lack of nitrogen, which I suspected, and then offers a lesson on botanical cross-breeding. Only 300 ancestral plants produced the many thousands of present varieties. (There may have been a gap of 20,000 years between the fall of each seed from the beak of a bird.) At this point it's difficult to ascertain exactly what's indigenous. The plant cover below an altitude of 1,500 feet has been destroyed and replaced by introduced species. It may seem a matter of small importance whether the course of evolution is attributed to conditions found in the species or to conditions external to it. If we are considering human beings, though, the latter possibility lands us in Fatalism. Perhaps flowers are subject to Fatalism as well. Pollen, for example, taken by a bee from one species of flower and deposited on another species is entirely wasted. No propagation will ensue.

June 5. The slope on the makai side, close to the water, is my problem area. I favor the kahili but this slope gets too much wind for it, and the ironwood is still too young to hold the soil by the beach which has a tendency to blow away or be carried out by the tides.

The ironwoods. A row of them tall and spidery now across the edge of the place where it fell off into the sea. Behind me, Revere, old estate, went on. Without Julia. Without Hilton. Without enough nitrogen in its soil. Without Paul. Without me.

June 12. At last evening's discussion at the Society, Mr. C. asked what the trigonantae are doing here. I answered my best, saying that none of the species found in tropical America is found here but there are twenty or more other kinds that are. Mr. C. disinclined to accept my word but Hilton backed me. His strong interest in things Hawaiian complements mine.

I turned the pages. Bone-colored, under fading ink, they were covered mostly with the feathery botanical meditations of this missionary descendant who was thirty-eight when she married Hilton.

March 20, 1941. Household may be thrown into flux. Hilton has taken up a strange cause — a native child. He seems set on the idea of this "hanai", as he puts it. The word means "feeding-child". But "hanai" is for Hawaiians among their own relatives. I can't believe he can be serious about another child in this house! He so seldom finds time for Paul. We can't be parents to this girl.

May 25. Decided on the native hibiscus arnottianus for the mauka hedge. It has an uncharacteristic fragrance and the skin of the petals is satiny. Then a bright red stamen.

May 26. I am certainly too old for another child.

May 28. There is a rumor that she may not come.

June 1. Apparently the child is to arrive after all and what our responsibilities may be is quite unclear. Everything here will be too pale for her. Too bleached by the sun and the spray. Even I. The house looks like driftwood. The creatures that come out at night—the hermit crabs—look for a place to hide. "Every day in every way we are getting better and better." So I tell myself.

The sun vanished suddenly behind the Koolaus and Paul's mother's words disappeared. I turned my headlights on and pulled out into the one-lane road that circles Lanikai. Kit would have come out, tripped over the cat, found her plate of food, refused or accepted it, forgiven me, granted me her absolution by now. Or not.

And in my purse, the fragile notebook and a stone wrapped in a fresh ti-leaf pressed against each other carelessly.

SEVENTEEN

As I pulled into the garage, I heard a clap of thunder and the hard, metallic fall of rain.

When you first hear it after long, hot days, there is that sting, that wetness to the throat and eyes, that luxury of wet on skin that spells relief, relief. There's the tar smell of pavement, and the sound. Everywhere, rain brings its own sound, but in Hawaii there are heavy, battered leaves that shake and whip, roofs banging, and the ground, absorbent as a sponge, resounding like slapped skin. It felt as if a great canvas over us had ripped apart, a long gash spilling water everywhere.

Rain on screens. Rain on the glass. Rain streaming down the curled leaves outside. The rain fell on us, over us, around us, shutting out all other sounds, cutting us off from everyone, washing away our secrets in the night.

Kit, curled in her room, was listening to the din, smelling it, leaving her windows up over her bed so that she lay in all the splattering. When she fell asleep, I took the light, dry, crumbling notebook to my bed.

June 2, 1941. Why is this necessary? I asked H. He says he must do whatever he can. They are "floundering", he says. They have lost everything, religion and customs and land. Those of us who love this fading race must care for its children, he says. This is a test of my charity.

June 3. She's here. Called Mihana. And speaking pure Hawaiian. As if all the work of the last two generations— of my parents and grandparents—were for naught. A child so obstinate and without manners won't have much success here, I tell Hilton. From what I hear she has been dedicated—a practice you don't hear of any more. She's been "given" to Pele to be a seer. And now she's "given" to us. Of course rumor has it that she has a royal mother, was fathered by someone of our society. But she's just a girl from the north shore as far as I can see. I see no sign of anything but indulgence in her face. She is as wild as the "kiawe", as scratchy and unlovely. Hilton says she's seven or eight but she looks to be ten years old at least. Of course that's the way with native girls. Aka has fitted her with a muumuu but she tears it off, runs out of the house wrapped in nothing but a cloth. We've had to take the few things she brought (a calabash, a quilt, and a pathetic pair of shoes). But one can't have her flying about in the altogether. Little Paul watches her, staying carefully beyond reach. And what our responsibilities are is quite unclear.

June 4. The girl reminds me of nothing so much as a natal plum. Carissa grandiflora. Before I was out of bed this morning she came in with her bark-colored skin. I'll try my best for Hilton. I'll provide snowy sheets. If we're to train her that will be a start, because she is appalled, for example, that we sleep "with something over us that has been underneath..." —meaning the sheets. She lies, close to her door, on a pile of mats. My mother would mutter

148

about the "devices of native superstition" if she were alive. I'm thankful she doesn't hear the footstep of the child. Mihana doesn't sleep at all. I hear her pace and pace.

June 6. I was taught concern for individual redemption. If everything is predetermined, how is this possible? I must believe there is an evolutionary demand for brotherly love. Either that or merely a contest with Satan. Which means I am responsible for the actions of all those around me, as well as their circumstance, environment. Gardening.

July 16. If my figures are accurate, all the endemic species are the result of isolation. On a larger land mass, plants of one kind tend to maintain a type, suppress disorder. But on an island, inbreeding encourages strange tendencies. I had hoped Revere was so isolated that I could keep the indigenous species pure.

July 21. The child is ill (an inflammation of the throat). Stays on her bed. H. lies beside her like a father. Mrs. Luahi at the plantation says as a youngster Mihana was given the royal alani flower bath. She slept for ten nights on alani leaves and therefore is "chosen". I guess this is part of the dedication? She has "mana" or power. "The Old Ways," Mrs. Luahi says. Mrs. L. insists we must not allow Mihana to dance. She is Hawaiian herself, and no doubt superstitious. She swears the power of the hula, associated as it is with Laka and Pele and the old ways, is so strong it can't be "dabble with". In other words, she really believes there is some dark potential there. When I smiled, she said, "That's why when something bad happen."

July 25. I fear H. becomes foolish over the child. He never leaves her side. After the wildness of her upbringing she should be "sensitized", he says. It will take some effort to soften her. Her feet, like little hoofs, can walk on anything. He says her mind, as well, must be reshaped, come under his influence. Perhaps at heart he is one of us—not so much a businessman—but a missionary—more like my father than I thought.

July 26. We work on word games, Scrabble, but she's skittish and hops about, runs to the window, laughs or looks bored. I don't have the interest. Or skill. Paul is still too small—I'll try her on hymns—a good tool for vocabulary work.

July 30. The garden is in disrepair. My notes always ne-glected. But Hilton is baffling. Close as we are here to the sea, he now denies her access to it. He says he fears "a pull". [Here something brutally scratched out.] *He wants a life for her less amphibious than that of her ancestors. Her "port of call" will be the bathtub, and from now on he will take her there each afternoon, he says. The example of his hand will teach her patience and cleanliness and she will soften in the process. But her temper is quite ferocious.*

Aug. 5. I must say it's surprising. She knows her plants. "Kukui" for example. Used for fishing, she told me when I took her for a walk; the kernels are roasted first then spat over the water to make it clear. Soot from the burned "kukui" nut can be used for dye as well. The inner bark of the tree makes a red stain. Then medicine: the sap from the green fruit cures thrush. On skin wounds it hastens healing. Leaves are a poultice. Roasted kernels are a laxative. She

went on and on in much the same vein for other plants.
Then I surprised her. I said what about "kukui" nut oil. For
lamps. She smiled at me for the first time.

Aug. 16. I heard Paul slapping her. My little jealous son.
She is such a child too, and physically quite small, but she
stopped him with a look. Little Paul was the one who burst
into wails and sobs.

Aug. 17. The bath. The treatment. Calm yourself, he says.
She yells and calls. He carries her back to her room. Does
he think I can't hear? The more I think of it, the more she
seems to be replacing something he has lost. I know it's not
unusual, this giving up of children. But the "hanai" system
usually goes on within families.

Aug. 17—Later. His own son is outside with the nurse
collecting ironwood cones. And he is inside with some
native woman's child.

At midnight I turned out the light and turned into the darkness of
my open, streaming window, Kit still apart from me, closed up
in her room. The mist that covered me and the drops that trickled
down my windowsill or were driven through the screen onto my
face were welcome. There is a saying here: rain never hurt the
old Hawaiians. The male sky is simply pouring himself into the
female earth.

Rain. We were shrouded in a wetness that cut off the mountains and made our small world smaller. In the night the land
stretched and moaned and sucked up the water that poured into

it, expanding, growing wider along the north shore of the big island. Pushing a heap of water away from it so that the shoreline of southeast Maui rose, and other island shorelines too. All of us rested on separate parts of this uneven, moving bed. I felt it in Kailua, where the water licked at the hem of the town. Someplace, Paul and Maya must have felt it too.

In the morning, cars wound slow progress around the Pali, nose to tail, inching through wind and rain as windshield wipers beat rhythmically to radio reports: "...two roads are closed in Waimanalo...the bridge is out between Frankie's Drive-In and Bellows Beach...", and children walked knee-high in puddles barefoot, umbrellas left behind so they came home from school mud-sliding, puddle-jumping, stained and dripping. Water was the only element.

Rain. In the afternoon, when it had knocked a tree down on our street, cutting off the phone and electricity, and when the street, lacking curbs and drains, was a river running between lights and signs and fences, I had a visitor.

I had been sitting around in a stupor of coffee and solitude, turning the brittle pages of the notebook, seeing the old scrawl become vague, listening to the slap of water on the tin roof, listening to the drumming overhead.

Aug. 24. Does he think I do not hear her cry across the quiet of an afternoon? Not tears—she doesn't shed them!—but a cry of something wounded. And there is our boy, standing, listening in the hallway.

Rain was still pouring from the opened sky, the swamp behind us sunk in an exotic flood of mud and metal. Birds gathering for shelter—Brazilian cardinals stumbling on water-heavy boughs, sparrows and finches clinging to dripping, heaving branches, doves on precise feet under bending trees. All nature taking cover. Even the Swamp Lady was heavy with rain. Even she was waterlogged. Rain was visited upon us. Then the only person left to share the meaning of events knocked on my closed front door.

Over the beating of the wind and rain, I yelled, "It's unlocked."

There was no roof over her, where she stood. Her hair was soaked. Her face was streaming with what I took to be tears.

"Maya." I stood up slowly, thinking, absurdly, that I'd missed her—that we could put our trouble out between us like a meal to be shared. And I was glad—glad that the tears or rain had made her face opaque. Glad, in spite of the rules of hospitality, to see signs of her misery.

Her hair was pulled back in garish red plastic barrettes and I was thinking that, under the film of tears, she looked quite ordinary, like any little girl who was ashamed and soaking wet, and how preposterous the scene was anyway.

She was dripping on my floor. "I'm sorry."

"All right. Come in." According to my mother, manners are the heart of civilized life.

She stepped back. Over the doorstep she wrung her hair out in her hand. "It never rains like this in summer."

Wrath of the gods. "Let me go get a towel."

Awkward suddenly, old, I turned and fled into the bathroom, grabbing a damp towel, my instinct toward hospitality at odds with my desire to punish this unhappy child.

The woman who stole Daddy's here, I might have said to Kit, passing her closed bedroom door. Oh do sit up. Come out and play. Maya of the honey skin, dove voice, treacherous heart. Has come to pay a call.

Locked away, Kit was still in her gloom. With all the weather and the tin roof banging she hadn't heard our voices, and I left her where she was. Her door was often closed now. It fit the mood of injury between us.

In the living room Maya was sitting in her tears, her shoulders shaking convulsively. I couldn't look at her. "What have you done with Paul?" I said. I almost added, my sole support, the father of my child, the man I love. My husband's child-lover was only a few feet away. She sobbed. Her teeth were chattering. I wrapped the yellow towel around her like a cape.

"What happened?" I already knew.

"He just..."—she choked—"...sent me away."

I wasn't ready. I said, "He's probably afraid...." Afraid of wanting you? Afraid of Mihana, of losing the little inheritance he had?

"I guess." She didn't believe this. She looked abandoned.

"He just said, 'Leave me! Go home.' That's all." She crumpled in my hands. "But I thought I could come here. I thought you'd understand how I feel." She put a hand up to my face, touching it, her fingers sticky, small, unclean, her clothes muddy and soaked.

I patted her and rubbed her back. He's having second thoughts, I said to myself. At least they're apart. At least, here, I know where she is. I smoothed her wet hair. "There are jeans in my closet. They'll be way too big for you. And that shirt you like. You want a beer?"

At this Maya, who was too young to drink, shook her head and began crying again.

I made tea. Returning, I found Maya holding Kit on her caned bed and rocking her. I stood there watching, rooted, unbelieving as I'd been the time Kit almost drowned in someone's swimming pool. Watching her, frozen, as she sank and rose up slowly to the surface, as if she'd been waiting to find Maya there.

Kit's room had taken on a hopeless look after her days alone in there, as if I had forsaken her, expected no recovery. But now with Maya on her bed Kit, in her ignorance, was smiling again.

"Come to the table then," I said. I poured Kit juice and found the last remains of some Portuguese sweet bread. Each of us had one piece, eaten relentlessly, the crumbs picked from our plates, the fingers licked clean. Maya bent over Kit, she wore her like armor. Kit was her friend. She had put on a pair of my jeans that were too long and a shirt she often borrowed when she stayed with us. Her hair had fallen from the red barrettes and damp strands framed her starchy face. I stared at her. Angrily. Maternally. She looked away, and in between us stretched the table I had cleared, now bare of everything except my elbows, as if we'd eaten from it human sacrifice instead of bread.

"Where were you anyway?" Kit asked.

"On Molokai," Maya said quietly.

"With my dad?"

"Yes. There's a pool there and a waterfall. The pool has a lizard goddess. It's a neat island."

Kit fell asleep as we ate and Maya carried her away like an insect staggering under the weight of something of its own kind and size. Then for a while, perhaps tucking Kit in, she left me alone again.

Outside it was becoming evening. Dusk gathered stars across the window like small pearls across the neck of darkness. The rain had stopped. I slid the window back and stood looking out. Maya crept back into the living room. With Kit in bed, it was time for us to talk.

Somewhere behind the downpour of rain the sun had fallen into the black sea. July was almost over.... Beyond the fig tree and the bushes in the yard the ocean smell was rich and heavy, full of sex. Out there somewhere, small lights moved on the water close to shore, roped to night fishermen who labored in the tides in rubber boots, casting their nets and lines out, catching small, innocent, blind fish.

A two-lane highway wound its long thread up the coast and on one side of it the cane fields stretched away in the evening darkness, miles and miles of them. Here Hilton had once worked. And Julia's father, too. One as a manager. One as an owner. Mihana had been born on this long coast, child of the night, night bloom. The cane fields wrapped around the Mill of Sorrows where, a century before, another child had fallen into a vat of molten sugar. After that the stones of the old mill had crumbled to black lace against the sky.

Sugar replaced Hawaiian staples like taro and yams. The ancient fishponds were condemned. Sugar ate up the land, even Revere, where sugar people, Needhams and Quills, had been the inheritors. Except for Paul and now he was joining them.

Along the highway, fruit stalls would be deserted for the night. These would be broken-down shacks with handwritten signs that promised mango for a quarter. There would be painted arrows pointing to tin cups. Black dogs would be chained to black trees and posts, barking a passage through the hollow night. People would play guitars and ukeleles. There would be singing and dancing and drinking and fights. Grown women are divided into wives and secrets, Mother always said. We are each of us predictable. That was my daily bread. Tell me, I said to Maya in my thoughts. Why did you even wait for me to leave? Tell me how you postponed your nights with him? They were enchanted, weren't they? Your sex was neither sweet nor violent; it was declarative and true. You wandered on the faceless hills and into the dark part of some dark valley, finding your way up to a deep, black pool. And did you ask the guardian *mo'o*, lizard goddess, permission to swim, dropping a leaf in the pool? While you and Paul climbed through gray light, he was still wrapped in disregard.

Our daughter was growing, passing through us like a shadow, like a cloud, while he missed the whole point. While he climbed into your arms, your body swelling, iridescent, while he climbed through the gray light. He missed the point. And in the nights while I thought that he was lost to me, while our child's sparrow bones moved next to me, lengthening steadily, I dreamed of you and missed the point.

And the sun-drenched trees offered you welcome. You were alive, grown up for the first time. You wanted him, to taste him so that he would live in you. And you were sensible when you made love; your wanting him became so powerful a thing that you preferred him to your sleep and, lying beside him, drew in, chewed up, and digested each night sound. Didn't you? Following dogs through late night wandering and keeping track of clock hands and moon set, you blessed what brought him...blessing both promise and reward.

By morning you were tired and ethereal, in a weird balance between love and disbelief. You'd learned his face, hair, voice, and pulse. You'd become beautiful for him. The heart you'd given him had been electric. And everything you did and failed to do was absolute. You had decided your own fate.

What are you doing here with me, under the sky, under the tree, under my hand? Tell me.

Suddenly Maya stood behind me. "I might be young now but I won't always be," she said.

"In the south," I said, "the slaves slept in white women's pearls at night to make them shine. Did you know that?" She must have hated being drawn to me for comfort, drawn because I was Paul's wife, Kit's mother, her mother's friend. Where is my husband? I wanted to scream. Where did you go with him? But I could not give her even that much.

How did you manage it? I might have said, but instead I asked, "What kind of girl would steal a grown man from his happy home?"

Standing at the window, Maya glared. "You think I had to steal his affection?" she asked, tapping on the thin glass of our mutual politeness. She moved her hips and ran her hands down them. "No way."

She sniffed at the dampness outside, which had begun to rise out of the earth, carrying with it the fumes of the plants and minerals. "The rain's all *pau*," she said, glancing at her hands and at the door. She clenched her fists, then she unclenched them and turned back to the room.

Moving like a small wild animal — elegant, weightless—she went to the chair Paul had occupied two weeks before. Now I could see that she was beautiful. She was beautiful in a way she'd never been. But it was ridiculous, of course, this rage of admiration.

"If you want to know, your chair's up in the rafters in the garage," she said tentatively, a child again, offering to please. "Your rocking chair. I can get it down for you. No problem at all."

When we first arrived Maya was my guide. It was early summer then and she was out of school so she went with me in my car to the Safeway where the other housewives shopped and to the hardware store for home-maintenance supplies. She knew what I would need—a hose for the garden, hammer and nails, a broom and a mop.

Then over the summer she showed Kit how to enter, with dignity, Punahou's first grade. She had done it once herself, she pointed out, and it was still her school. When fall arrived she accompanied Kit on the city bus. It was a private school and Maya's enrollment there, as well as Kit's, was part of the generosity of Hilton's will.

I followed her out to the garage and watched her swift hand-over-hand into the rafters—turning the walls of the garage into a jungle gym. What a place to put my rocking chair, I thought. Paul never liked it very much, but I nursed Kit in that chair. We brought it across the ocean with us. I know every groove of it against my back and my behind.

Once it was reinstalled, it was Maya who rocked into the fast approach of darkness, magnetically pulled to the chair or to keep me out of it.

We might have sat there wordlessly for ever. For a long while I couldn't think of what to say to her. We sat in a room that held our jealousy and blame. Then I said, "What good would his love do you anyway? It isn't real. It doesn't even start to be real love."

She crossed her ankles in a way that irritated me, rocking, rocking.

"He loves me all right," she stated confidently, looking straight ahead, fingering the pearls I imagined at her neck. Is this alienation of affection? Is this affection alien? She gestured around her, taking in my room, my house. "It started here, you know. While you were gone."

"Spare me. It doesn't matter now."

"No. I mean we were working on your house. For you. Paul wanted to do that for you."

While I defended, mentally, each corner of the room, she went on, "It's nice now. You like it better, don't you?"

"You changed everything," I said flatly.

"I changed too," she said.

Your change be damned, I thought. How does it measure up to mine? A child to my credit and twelve years of married life. There was a bottle of wine on the bookcase and I uncorked it viciously. The tightness in my jaws was painful and my stomach ached. But it was not without its pleasure, all this fierce anxiety. I poured the wine. "Why don't you go back to Mihana? She's all upset, you know." Suddenly solicitous, and aware that there were advantages to me in holding her there. I didn't believe her for a minute, didn't believe it was over, but she was with me and not with Paul, so if he wanted her back he'd have to take her from me, and if he wanted to come home he'd have to declare himself in front of her. I knew what I wanted from Maya. I wanted Paul from Maya only because he didn't want her. Not any other way.

"She'd be mad that I came to you but I don't care. She thinks I'm with Paul anyway. She's not clairvoyant you know. I want to stay here. She might kill him or something if he turned up at Revere. Is it okay? If I stay here with you?"

She drank her wine. "When I said I was sorry at the door, I didn't mean I'm sorry," she went on in a rush. "I meant I was sorry about the mess." She tipped back in her chair. "But he was—so gentle!" She closed her eyes and actually licked her lips.

"It's a mess all right." Then I added, to shock her out of her adult sophistication, "Just where did you make it exactly? Here on my floor? Or in my bed?"

"We asked him over the night you left," Maya answered easily. She opened both her hands at this—the local sign of a shrug. "To the house."

As if it were just any house, inhabited by any family. "Which of you asked him over though? Your mother? Or did you?"

She shrugged again. She looked through the screen doors, seeing my garden lit by a spotlight that she or Paul had fastened under the tin roof. My asparagus fern in its torn plastic pot, its fronds hanging almost to the ground, moved in the air, silvered and feathery under the light. Moths darted about. A gecko waited, alert on the glass. Maya's attention span was fairly short. She sat sucking a finger and looking out.

"Go on!" I demanded. "Tell me whose fault it was." She was innocent, too young, I thought, but she had opened the shirt she wore and was idly scratching her breast. Then she began, as if I cared, as if I wanted ordered recitation of the facts. I wanted to know how it felt, and how they touched and what they said. Tell me the way he looked at you, I thought. Tell me the way he saw you in his mind, the way you touched him through the strangeness of not knowing, because I can't feel that.

Tell me, I thought, about that.

And did Paul worry when he held you the first time? Was he extreme or gentle? How would you know? After all is said and done. This kind of thing is relative. Tell me, how did you manage this, how do you measure this, I thought.

And I sat back and listened to her and left my glass of wine untouched.

So it began, a curious, dull recitation of a desire so intense it left them blameless, overtaken by events. "I cleaned the house.

Mihana let me try her nail stuff." She held a red nail up for me to see that the color, at least, had survived all this. "And I changed my hair. Mihana made a bed for him. We ate. They drank. And when I fell asleep, she told him to carry me away." She smiled to herself.

"Away from her?" The woman who slept on *alani* leaves for power when she was a child. The woman who was not supposed to dance or dabble, and who made potions for cures.

The cat came in and rubbed against my leg. He nudged my arm. She would have gone on talking if I'd left the room, once she'd begun, or if I'd left the house and driven the car to town. In that blank monotone, she would have gone on. I was her listener, her witness, and she was turning Paul into a legend as she spoke. She was lulling me, her legs pulled up against her in my rocking chair, the chair balanced at a forward tip. She put her head down on her knees. "I hope he doesn't suffer too much."

I couldn't stop. "But did it happen that first night?"

"He wants to marry me, he told me so. He told me anything else is wrong. I'm young but I won't always be and he's not so old and one day he'll take me back to Revere and I'll eat up his sadness. I'll do anything, anything for him."

The gecko on the screen moved, darted, and froze again. From inside, if you go up close to them, you can see their hearts beating through their thin, transparent skin.

She looked at me. Still innocent. "What do you think he's going to do?" She had begun to cry again, but she was laughing too and I looked away.

"You can stay. I'll go fix you up a place to sleep."

Paul's room would put her closer to him, farther from me. She'd make a nest among his few remaining things. But she'd be here, under this roof, and not with him—not as it must have been that night—Maya on her salty bed, under the white mosquito net a million years ago, young and perfect, carried to her room. Paul putting her on the bed like a dead princess. Looking at her. Taking her hair apart, unbuttoning the fastenings that ran the long length of her dress.

But she was rocking and laughing and hugging her knees.

"What is he going to do?" she giggled, and sobbed simultaneously. "When is he coming? I miss him so much."

Seeing her turn into a crazy, chattering savage, I went out and closed the door.

EIGHTEEN

Maya had belonged to me—a kind of baby sister—longer than she'd ever cared for Paul, and now I closed the door on her and went to bed.

Aug. 26, 1941. Hilton says she eats quite nicely now (they take their meals together) and learns to spell. Perhaps the Scrabble after all. Last night I heard them in the bath. I wonder if I'll ever believe she belongs.

Aug. 27. One can't imagine a more pathetic sound than that of this young native child. She has to be locked up in her dark room to calm her down.

Aug. 29. The question is what pace to take. If this process of conditioning and reeducation is sound, it's as if Hilton carves his image on her flesh. It's as if he tries, every afternoon, to break new ground. But something else. I'm aware of this. That she is telling him things. And he is interested. And he is learning from her.

Aug. 30. I think the area makai of the lava wall is the place for a run of lantana. I like the peculiar smell of it—weedy and tough—and the multiple colors. But Mr. Y. tells me a mutation of it has spread from the Manoa–Palolo ridge until it covers large areas of the valley and seems to be subverting native forms. Resistance to parasites?

Sept. 3. If there is only one possible outcome for any circumstance then the course of all history is predetermined. No effort can affect the result. If we cannot change our circumstance without action and the action is already predetermined by our circumstance then we are only vessels, we are only instruments.

Sept. 5. I've been thinking back to my girlhood. Before the teaching. Before marriage. Before motherhood. The time I went back to teachers' college on the mainland was the only time I've been away. I remember standing at the rail on the ship's deck, our first night out, looking over the side to see the phosphorus on the water, which I had never seen before. Even now I can't see phosphorus without qualms of conscience. I knew then if I could I would turn back that night. I had a ready-made dress for that trip made of blue serge. I also had a white morning dress with green dots of which I was very proud. Before this, Mama made all my clothes. I couldn't go back until I had my certificate. I wanted to be like Mama and teach at Punahou.

Sept. 8. I'm at a loss. Where this child takes us—into what regions of the human or prehuman spirit—I can't guess. I watch as he shuts himself away with her, and still I swear it's little Mihana that guides the way.

Sept. 12. Is this my own journey or do I travel on someone else's?

Maya had moved into the house. Waking, I'd hear her in the kitchen, knowing which one of us I was because I could remember more of my own past than hers. She was the other part of me. She loved my husband, fed my child, and left little offerings at my door for me. I'd find a mug of coffee where the lamp had been, next to my bed, and lie there drinking it and watching morning happen to the room: a wedge of sunlight broadening, moving across the wall, picking out objects in its path to cast them in its light, after a moment releasing them and moving on. The clutter on my bureau briefly benevolent—each thing examined for its moment and then abandoned as I had been. It had seemed possible at one time for some moment in my life to stand out like that—a moment with spark and definition.

And if she wanted to take care of me? Why not? While we waited for my husband to come home. The sunbeam had settled, however briefly, however temporarily, and for the moment it was mine. One morning, tapping on the bedroom door, Kit looked in behind a cookie on a blue and white plate. "We made the batter early while you were still asleep." While I was reading your grandmother's sad heart, I thought, closing Julia's book.

The sunlight had been stretching lazily toward where she was standing and now it grabbed her hair and I reached out, too, pressing my fingers into its warm softness, its smell and feel changed since that first indecent luxury of smelling at a baby. The smell had changed, no longer mine or even hers. Now the straight hair of anybody's child nuzzled against me, pushed up against my angularity, testing the pleasure and acceptance I would muster while the soft brown cookie on the plate between us scattered crumbs on the quilt and sheets.

Once I had been unashamed with her, feeding her from my breasts; we were almost allied. The happy calm of infant next to me, bound to me, bound me to earth. I was significant; a middle point. Once the being next to me absorbed the smallest inferences and minutest implications of my body, sending me back its own; we woke together, joined like perfect love. She knew my humor. I knew hers. Flesh bond remarkable. No father ever knew that hold.

Once I had known exactly what she wanted; once I had been the thing she wanted until, stiffening, she pulled away, already setting out on her own extreme course. That morning in my bed, I held her for moments during which we breathed in unison again, sensing the sweet fatality of every breath, the mortality of Kansas nights.

I ran my hand along Kit's spine, measuring its terrible fragility, and knew that my intentions couldn't armor her—the frame, the skull, the life so valuable and unprotected beneath airy skin.

Outside, birds were announcing claims and there were morning sounds of someone starting up a lawn mower, of someone else starting up a car. Before the day squeezed us into its fist, I held Kit close, noticing the sounds and smells with something like old pleasure. Kit and I lifting courage from the plate, and crumbling it on my bed.

Sept. 15. My mother used to sing a hymn about a sick boy visited by a dove.

> *He must be pure and good and kind*
> *Must strive and watch and pray*
> *For unresisted sin at last*
> *Will drive that bird away*

Sept. 16. War war war. Outside this house that's all anyone will talk about! We are told to buy black curtains as if something dies in us after dark.

Sept. 17. This morning I let her out and walked her in the garden and I took my Paul. Mihana showed no interest, only wanted to talk in her broken English about the "cure plants". I promised her I will plant certain things. She took my hand. She is now so docile. He calls this training. But what I think I should not say.

"I dreamed I met you at a fork in the road," Maya said, when I got up and went into the kitchen. "Standing under a tree. You were waiting for me."

Like hell, I thought. What I am waiting for is Paul. I now had Maya in my mind exactly where I wanted her. We were a perfect pair, her youth as skilled as my experience. I'd heard her rustling and shaking like a small dog in the dark. I'd heard her sounds. Once I had gone in quietly and stood and watched.

Sometimes Maya played with Kit, sometimes she sat with me. Maya and I sat outside on the lanai, drinking iced tea. Direct descendants of women who had suffered everything already, we had our futures to consider, and we considered them.

Maya was caught like a thief, her small hands, her fragile face, her skinny knees, between childhood and adulthood. Her voice changed and her skin changed. Her hoarse laugh grew self-conscious so she used it less. Once she approached Kit. "Can I play?"

Kit was combing the hair of her favorite Barbie doll. "I can't find the brush. Did you take it?"

"For what?"

"For who cares! To use, *lolo*." The word for stupid, crazy.

167

"Oh yeah. Sure!"

"Where are your Barbies anyway? Why didn't you bring them over with you?" Kit ran the comb through the creature's hair. She was crouched over. Maya crouched in front of her.

"You want me to go home and get?" Slipping into pidgin.

Kit peeled the clothes off her doll abruptly, with one stroke of her hand. "Take it. This one's yours. You can have it." She thrust the naked doll at Maya savagely.

"No way...." Maya dropped the hand she had raised to receive Kit's gift.

"I thought you wanted to play though!" Kit burst out, thrusting the tiny silver dress at Maya. Nothing was clear to her.

Sept. 20, 1941. The story is perfectly well known out here. That earth is mother. An old belief. Old as heaven. And heaven is father. A daughter is born to earth and heaven. I hear them practising the name, saying it slowly though her tongue stumbles over it. Hoohokukalani. The father takes his own child, and with her produces the first ancestor, the first chief. This happens on Oahu. He tells her this story.

Sept. 22.
I must strive and watch and pray
For unresisted sin

Sept. 28. A woman came to my door. She said she was from the North Shore. She told me she wanted to see his child. Squeamish, I told her little Paul was napping. She said, "The other one. If she does all right here. I wanted to know."
I wouldn't speak to God of this if I believed in Him.

Oct. 3. Last night in bed, I thought, "Perhaps this is my own notion, perhaps I got this up myself," perhaps that is not what the woman meant, or perhaps it wasn't true. But if it is—and there is this curious relationship—how shall I bear it? I even prayed for ignorance, to be "blind and slow of mind". I decided I was mistaken and, anyhow, I have had no proof.

But today I have asked Mrs. Luahi. It is true. Between father and daughter here, or between brother and sister, it is a very old traditional thing. It is sacred, in fact, for those of high birth.

Mrs. Luahi says the woman is called the North Shore woman. Everyone knows of her.

Oct. 10. Consider the hibiscus. Consider the wind that tears it and the pests that gnaw at it. Which does God love? If He loves them equally, if He loves the sparrow and the hawk, then He loves chaos. What good is that?

Oct. 11. In the beginning, Mother Earth married Father Sky. The father imposed tabus so that he couldn't sleep with his wife on certain nights. Instead he slept with his child. That's how the race of chiefs began. And this is the highest marriage here, he tells her. Father and daughter. Brother and sister. I heard him say those words.

Oct. 12. And the lion with the lamb shall lie down together. Even the lion with his cub. I know what he does to her. How is it called among the civilized? Horrible beyond anything. White violence. White lies.

169

Oct. 14. My only memory is of passivity. Is of a voyage undertaken by others, conducted by others, on which I am a passenger, as if I sat down at a feast that I had not cooked and was not invited to. And if the table's set with vile secrets? If I am spying at a loaded table, where do I report?

Nov. 30. "There is eternal virtue in silence."

I put the frail notebook down, suddenly sure that Maya was Paul's sister. Paul and Maya, I thought, over and over, Paul and Maya. Then like a dog I ran outside and in the darkness, against the side of the house, I cried and heaved up the dinner I had just eaten. And wept again. They were siblings. If he came back and gave her up without knowing that, though, it would be out of love for me.

NINETEEN

I was concentrating. I was engaged, remember, in necessity. In the buying of things to eat and wear and use, in the using and wearing and eating of them. I couldn't save the cat from heavy wheels, the counter-top from burning coffee spill. Or Maya's hope. I wounded each day with my beating against it. There was a war on. None of us was that eager to grow up.

I went out and came back and waited. Maya persisted in belief. Hers was the blue flower not yet born.

Sometimes I roused myself enough to sweep the floor or wash the dishes from a meal or iron one of Paul's shirts again so I could have the sensation of doing something. For him.

"What's it like, doing that all the time?" Maya asked me jealously one afternoon, while I sprinkled a shirt with water from a bowl, waving my hand over it as if granting it absolution.

"Nice," I said, sniffing at the armpits, and buttoning the front tenderly. She touched the buttons of her own shirt absently, and turned away.

She thought about him all the time and smelled him at times, next to her. Whereas I told her I'd forgotten him; my vigil was unconfessed. I waited secretly. Kit, playing with the cat in her nightgown, or skating down the street, had found a better way to wait. Grown women spend their lives with both hands on the clock: to be found, to be taken, someone come, this is the only dance I know, please stay. Lives that wring out of us the call of ancestors, lives that make the room we live in our own flesh. When a false note is struck, we make a backward rush, that's all, into a place we have forgotten. We become faithful and persistent. We don't ask, what will I be left, where will it end? We make the backward rush.

TWENTY

Of course I understood. Perfectly. Mihana. Ten-year-old child. Eight-year-old child. Twelve. Unbleeding still, with her fresh wound. Accepts the little pain because he ministers to it. He comes each day to minister to it.

He draws her tenderly into his ample lap. She's in her shift of hand-stitched cotton, the one Aka has sewn for her, or sometimes only in white underpants because she has no shame.

He draws her into his big lap at these times—times which are separate from her lessons and his sternness. And he is a forgiving, kindly father, anxious for her pleasure. He is tenderness itself. He touches the edge of her finger or her ear, for she is sensitive in these places, and asks her about her dreams and imaginings.

I am Wakea, he tells her.

I am a princess, she says.

And he agrees.

It is an understanding between them that she never mentions fear.

The consideration he shows her inside her room is separate from their relationship outside. It has to be this way. He is here to assuage that part of her that has been hurt out there in the larger house. At first she resists; she fights like a threatened cat, all claws and growls. But how can she argue with this kindness? It is the only one in her narrow, enclosed life.

Between two o'clock and four o'clock in the afternoon, before tea and during the daily household rest, he enters her small shuttered and locked room, showing her at these hours so much tenderness that finally the room will be unlocked for good, for where else would she go? After the mornings of training, after the rest periods full of understanding, where would she go?

She is seven or eight when he first comes to her. What section of her body brings him pleasure at such youth? The skinny thighs? The hollow calves? Unopened buds of breast? The unfuzzed, candid genitals? From which he sucks like nectar pleasure stolen from the petals she does not know she possesses. No one's warned her about this.

At first, as I said, he brings her to his ample lap, stroking the child-skin of her bare back, also her face, licking the corners of her eyes to clear the tears away, an understanding human animal.

It is her mother's touch she misses most. The way her mother undressed her for a bath. It is her mother's touch she seeks in this—gentle reproaches for skinned knees, her unwashed ears, her wild, unbrushed hair. The gentle taking off of clothes as if to free her for a warm swim in her ocean and a cool sleep on her mat.

He takes her to her bath and washes her the way a mother does, clucking a little at her alarm when the spittle gathers on his lips. Reproaching her. And scrubbing her. Then taking her in to her bed and opening her thighs and drying her. The fear and shame she hides under the rough touch of the towel silence her now on shuttered sunlit afternoons with him causing her to lie still lie still lie still as earth to bring the old man his relief.

He may be a god, you know, her mother said, they come here, swallow us, and cause our dreams to be of heaven, of new chiefs and kings.

Her tears are taken on his tongue to her small nipples, to her buttocks, to the place she hides from him. She is a traveled river, ditch of tears. Her tears connect her, stick her together, glue her together, keep her together in one piece. She comes to know herself this way, thinking that tears and pleasure always match, that by entering fear and pain she holds herself together in the midafternoon heat of that coastline inhabited by men. White men or gods who own her mother and the land and the water that irrigates the land and the food that is grown on the land, and the sandalwood and the sugar cane and the men who make the planks and her mother and her house and everything. Men with so much power that to find yourself needed by one of them is a revelation. To find yourself needed by a man who uses your tears to bring moisture to his mouth so he can take you apart and put you together again is an education in itself. Your tears are a libation. They make it possible for him to open you and plant in you the silky, fat stalk of himself.

When the child Paul is heard in the hallway or outside in the garden, the old man loses heart. It is his child—boy child—smaller and noisier and more alone. Then the old man grows limp; he forgets his need. The moisture on his mouth is unpleasant. His smell against you is rank and sour. Then he turns to you. You are my child, he whispers, my little princess, and you are more powerful than anyone else. These are the words he's never said to you before. These are the special sounds between you, your new language, and you come to believe in them because of their intensity. To believe, especially, that you are his child. Forsaking all others, is what he says.

That he also planted himself in your mother at the plantation and watched her grow big with you and resisted the impulse to pluck you up the way he raised and watched and resisted the sugar cane until it was time, you understand.

That he sees you as the fruit of himself, green mango clinging to the branch, fit only for salt, too bitter and unripe to give away, you understand.

That your mother kissed you and fed you and bathed you more carefully, more sadly every year, you understand.

You come to believe this, and to remember the day you were handed to him by your mother, with a quilt and a pair of shoes.

You believe this when he draws the fabric away from your waist and across your bony hips and over your thighs as if it is a skin to peel away. You believe this when he tastes you and says you are fruit and wraps you around himself like his own flesh. When he licks the corners of your eyes and the petaled flesh between your legs you believe you belong to him, for who but a parent would taste your flesh?

And when that other child is heard stumbling in the garden or waiting outside in the hallway, you shudder and sigh. You close your eyes and your nostrils and wait for the troubling child to pass and for the man who needs you to say, you are my magic one. You are the earth. I am the sky.

You accept his fingers as you do his voice. You accept the pain that the turn of his hand in your body brings because his hand makes everything you know and you accept the mass of his softer flesh, the thing he pushes into you, because you have no choice and because it is easier than the hand which he turns and because he talks to you. You close your eyes to the sight of him and the smell of him grows familiar and he touches you until the wooden louvers on the window fold over you like the wings of insects. He says words to you. The only kind words that you know.

The other people in the house are unimportant to you both. You only wait for them to leave you alone in one way or another so that the power can be given and received without interruption.

You are the focus of all his strength, you must begin to take this for granted. That your performance, your training and pleasure, are important to him you must believe. It begins to seem natural.

And that the other child is sent away. Everyone in the house is sent away. The old woman dies. There is only the old man and you.

And he tells you the story that is well known out here. That earth is mother. An old belief. Old as heaven, which is Lani. Father or heaven, means the same thing. Like where you live. Heavenly place, Lanikai. A daughter is born to earth and heaven and the father lies with her. And with his daughter he has many children. The ancestors. This happens on Oahu. This first, this original most special, most precocious love.

But not for many years do you understand the power that comes from your hours of fear and humiliation. The old man is ashamed of his obsession. He knows that it sets him apart. That he cannot help himself. And you know this is the power he's given you. Allowing you to see him in a state of need you do not share.

What occurs between you is not commerce, but the bestowal of gifts. You give him the pleasure of your body, year after year, from the time you are seven or eight or ten. He gives you, at last, his milk-skinned child, Maya. And he gives you Revere for her.

TWENTY-ONE

Revere looked empty, unguarded, as I drove in. The house was dark. A dog howled. There was no one on the lawn or in the hall. So I pushed on, barefoot, the way Mihana always was, making no sound, feeling the breath of the house — old and wheezing on every part of my skin.

What was it like growing up in this place? When Julia died? Who held Paul and talked to him? Who taught him to crawl and walk and swim? Not Hilton. It must have been Mihana, always older, braver—always ahead of him, always inviting him.

How did his days go then? Did he sit and wait for her to come and play, jealous and wondering, as she had what she called her "teaching time" with Hilton? Mihana didn't go to school, even if he did. There was no need.

But when the two of them were children again in the afternoons, didn't he follow her into the jungle, where she showed him how to climb trees, how to mud-slide, how to find *lilikoi* to eat, and how to hide? Didn't he follow her when she led him down to the beach? He had told me that one day he dug a deep hole in the sand and buried her, leaving a breathing space and then erasing even that, amazed that she didn't resist—and running far back up to the house, where she was waiting for him, having escaped. He never got over that.

Outside someone was tapping on a gourd or drum. The dog was moaning in the background, softly, as if to accompany the sound. The sitting room was dark, but a light from outside threw the figure of Mihana on the blind, projecting onto it her elegant movements—slow and serene. She was lifting her arms, bending elbows and wrists; her fingers were holding invisible things. It was the most sensuous movement, even in shadow, that I had ever seen. She was huge on the blind—immense, like the old Hawaiian queens. For the first time I saw what she might have been. Mihana lifted her arms and bent her knees, taking small, sliding steps. On the vast lawn beyond the blind she moved elaborately. She lifted her arms and danced and flowers spilled from her shoulders as she moved and from her hair and from her hands and from her clothes.

The night-blooming cereus that grew beside her on a wall opened petal after petal, slowly, as she turned her hand or bent her wrist—as if it had saved itself for a night like this when, like a visitation, buds would appear along its bumpy branches and open up into sudden, waxy, deep-cupped flowers.

I stood looking at Mihana's shadowy form through the blind. There was only the sound of the jungle around us now, of insects and frogs keening, and the rhythmic tapping of a gourd.

Someone was playing it—perhaps it was Paul. Maybe he and Mihana were here together waiting for Maya to come back. Perhaps, in time, she would. I wouldn't blame her. A place like this and Paul. It seemed entirely possible that he was there, tapping his palm against a dried gourd rhythmically. It seemed I must confront both of them with Mihana's treachery, with not telling me and with tempting Paul and with using her daughter the way she had been used. I felt outraged at the thought of Mihana's dance. She was not supposed to dance—and I'd never seen her do it before. And it was so persuasive...but I rushed out through the door that opened to the lanai. I broke into the night, slamming my hands against the darkness and screaming, "You knew all the time!"

I checked the whole area of darkness, where only Mihana stood close to the small transistor radio. There was no sign of Paul.

Mihana bent down and turned off the ancient sound of gourds. "How is she doing with you?" she asked quietly. "My child?" Then she added, "You must understand. For them it is something very strong. It is beyond them, this kind of love. It is sacred in fact. It is beyond them at this time."

At that moment she looked only sympathetic, patient, lonely—a lonely woman who was losing hold of her child, who missed the caretaking of her—but I spat out, "I'm keeping her away from here. She's innocent. Do you get my point?" My voice rang through the jungle. The trees, the grass, the tired hibiscus and *uluhi* and succulents, the night-blooming cereus with its watery scent—they were all indifferent. The house was black as I went back inside. But I retraced my steps. I counted them...ninety, eighty-nine, eighty-eight...all the way to the door. Revere seemed hideous. I wanted to go home to Maya. To see her sleeping on the mattress in Paul's room, on the newly laid mats.

TWENTY-TWO

Maya and I were together now as I had wanted us to be. I would protect her. Together, twins abandoned, we suffered from the same disease. We beat to the same heart. We shared an interest so common, we needed each other's company.

We sat together in the dusky sunlight of the house, breathing the same thick air but unaware of the same truth. I didn't say, it's your own blood you love. I didn't say, his touch is poison to you, child, it is a knife. I didn't say, this is the second curse, the second tabu. First, you must not kill your brother. Second, you do not dare make love to him.

We sat together in the heat of the day, the time of day when everything was quiet, when the streets and driveways, the yards and houses were deserted. When even the dogs, tied up or kept in small, fenced yards, were still.

Marines were practicing maneuvers. Their planes roared constantly over our house. The war was what everyone talked about. Perhaps they were bombing Kahoolawe with the Canadians, disturbing old gods. Soldiers everywhere. Training at every base. Flying out. Resting and recuperating afterward in Waikiki. Below the Marine base the giant Safeway sprawled empty and chill. Half of us in the neighborhood bought our groceries there. Half of us went to the Chinese store, Kalapawai—a small wooden shack partially painted red which reeked of salted, musky food, and which was deserted now. It was afternoon. Everything was still.

Before she went outside one afternoon, Kit found a cardboard box and packed her dolls away. The floppy baby doll she'd had since they were almost the same size, another one with handmade clothes from Kansas, and the Barbies — elongated surrogates with silver dresses and fur coats.

Into the box Kit packed the pictures Paul and I had always tacked up on her walls. Since she first held a crayon we'd moved them from rented house to rented house. The chimney, smoke, and slanted roof-windows. The closed door with mommy daddy kit and luke, large star hands fanning flatness. Staring eyes. Smiles. All of us.

Maya lay at my feet, the cat curled around her like a vine throwing off blossoms of ear, tail, and whiskers, opening an eye protectively. I lay on the battered sofa, as if I were Maya's guardian, as if I dreamed her dreams, through a week of afternoons, the room, affected by the clutter of our comforts, a mess of pillows, magazines, newspapers, books; our empty cups and glasses covering table-tops and floor. Being superstitious, I thought that if I focused on the teapot it would break before I picked it up. The penalty for my attention now was sure to be bad luck. The room was full of things that might be hurt by me or not.

I dreamed that Maya and I lay together in the bedroom of my mother's house. We talked contentedly. I touched her back. And every detail of the room was there, the dolls and books, the window seat and shelves, the heavy curtains shutting out huge trees. Trees we could step out on, staying aloft for days, for ever, growing tough and childlike, both of us springing from branch to branch. Aloft, out of reach, and under us the dry, enormous lake bed, a sea of grass and bones and fish.

"How did Hawaiians sacrifice?" I asked Maya.

"If somebody broke the *kapu*—like touched something he shouldn't have or went into a sacred place—then they gouged out his eye and killed him. Sometimes they ate the eye for strength."

"Eye for an eye," I said, looking at her. But it was for the gods, not just for law or for revenge.

The tide was out. Children had left the shores of their houses and front yards to spend the waning hours of the afternoon pulled far away from us. Later they would seep in again. Later we would stand up, facing each other in the middle of the mats—mats she had laid in this dark room. Both of us in brown shorts, barefoot, hearts in our hands.

Maya was matter of Paul's flesh, blood of his heart.

And where was Paul? Was he ashamed or afraid? Was he cowardly or brave? Which of us had failed? Or had he failed both of us? One day he and I had sailed together out beyond the reef and steered a straight course past Pearl Harbor. We were cold and the shore was unfamiliar. The mountains had no shape that I could recognize. I wasn't sure where we were, or what part of the island we had reached. I wasn't sure of anything but Paul, who told me when to duck my head or shift my weight.

"I'm going to swim," he told me then. "Keep your eye on the land. Keep the sail at right angles to it if you can. Aim for it. Okay? Let's see you steer this thing." And he leapt in.

All I could see of Paul was his raised arm. All I could see after he went into a wave was water and a distant line of land. And water that was magnetized. He was held down. I was pulled from his side. To steer a boat, he'd said to me, you mainly tack, you mainly head into the wind, that means you push the tiller out, and you look at the land. To change direction, he had said, release the leeward sheet, take up the weather sheet. Straighten the tiller first, he said. Do you see what I mean? Look at the line of land and keep the sail straight. I'm going to swim. You have to bring her about and slow her down—it's hard to get back on. And I had thought, why is he testing me this way? Now I thought, will

Maya fail him, or will I? All I could see from where I sat was water and the distant line of land.

When Kit came in at last that day she went straight to her room and held herself against the darkness, not even turning on her bedside light. Dusting her hands across the toys stacked on the shelves, peering into her bed which caught in its fold the sea light, she stood there waiting, like the rest of us, between the perfect day and our longest night. The sky was blue and green and gold. Somewhere the sun had become water-swallowed flame and Kit was unaware that I watched from the hall. She does belong here on this island, I thought bitterly. Like Maya and Paul.

Somewhere Paul held on like the long summer, while I threw ice water on my sheets to frustrate the spirit of heat that lay beside me. I heard the noise of something falling through the summer sky and raining down on me, the thud of something ripe that smelled as sweet as rot. The mangoes had begun to fall. And over me, the tin roof was receiving them.

TWENTY-THREE

One morning Kit answered the phone and yelled, "Mom, it's Daddy!" so happily into the summer air that Maya had to know. She must have sat up with a start, as Kit and I did, running our fingers through tangled hair, our pulses and our thoughts racing giddily. The call had come for me, though.

"I need to talk to you, as soon as possible, right now if you can manage it." Paul's voice at last. The same words as before.

"But where? Where are you now?"

"I'm at Revere. I just got here. I'll be at Pinky's in twenty minutes. I'll meet you there."

Which meant I had no time once again to fix things up in terms of clothes and face and hair. No time now to design the meeting.

It didn't take much time to get there. Nothing compared to the time it would take to get back home again. I was aware, pulling into the bare parking lot in midafternoon lull, that this time Paul must have his mind made up. He didn't want to confront Maya but he was coming back to me. That was why he had chosen Pinky's. Without Kit or Maya there, he could talk to me. I was prepared, therefore, to forgive everything, all at once.

The afternoon was gray, but there was a wind in from the ocean and the *hau* trees with their giant leaves like hands rustled hopefully. I had taken the main streets to the row of small buildings across from Safeway, close to the base. Our little town smelled salty, especially here where the sea turned in from Mokapu and forced itself on the land. Gravel turned under the tires softly as I drove in. Palm trees stirred. A local woman was passing with a baby in a stroller as I climbed out of the car. A pale blonde who must have been a military wife was just on her way out. I'd never been to Pinky's in the afternoon.

No wonder. It was dark and air-conditioned, grim. Whatever happened here was for the night. The place had a worn pool table, a boy polishing glasses behind the bar, a woman sleeping, legs straight out, in a booth. Adjusting to the change in air and light, I thought of the Blue Goose, where Paul had met me after school in my senior year. He was a legal drinker, older than my friends, and held his beer proudly as I leaned against him in our favorite booth hoping everyone would see us together. He had put the years of eastern school behind him; he had forgotten his dead mother and been forgotten by his father; he was studying photography; and we were going to run away as soon as we could.

Now he was sitting in the shadows of a dark booth, curled over a mug of beer, and he did not get up as I approached. We had long since dispensed with those formalities. Now I had nothing left to lean on and I stumbled awkwardly and reached out, as if to clutch the table or the air or my desire to have Paul in hand. He took a sip of beer at the wrong moment, making me want to apologize for him. I bent over and moved sideways into the huge turquoise plastic booth. He said something about the length of my hair, the look of the place, the time of day. Then he ordered another glass and a full pitcher. For us to share. I watched his left hand gesture to the boy with the towel in his belt and his right hand move the glass around in rings it had made on the dark wood. And while I watched Paul's hands I wondered why, as his wife, I found it so hard to look at his face. Was it his sins or mine between us? I couldn't tell. But the facts were finally assembling, sitting in witness in all the other booths around the room.

Pinky's was full of fish. The man who owned the place had glass tanks full of them everywhere. Behind us one bubbled and spluttered as if the fish might suffocate. Overhead were fishnets dripping with glass balls and dried lobsters and crabs. That afternoon the place had the gloomy look of a shipwreck; as if I'd been too hopeful, as if we were already sunk.

"I guess you're angry," he began.

"No." Not quite a lie. But everything depended on him. I wanted him to come back for love, for loyalty at least. The messenger, the bearer of bad news is killed. Why tell him about Hilton and Mihana now if he'd come to patch things up with me? "No. I'm okay."

"And of course it's your right to be mad. Your absolute right. If you want to spend time on that now, we'll go ahead. There's only one innocent party in all this. That's why I'm here.

"It's been the longest summer, ever, in my whole life, I'll say that," he went on, shaking his head as if the movement of the planets and his own stars baffled him. "Thank God it's almost over. Kit's school about to start?"

"A couple of weeks," I said tightly. He should know that much, at least. "Where have you been?"

"In limbo."

"What have you decided?" I could hardly bear to ask. I had no interest, any longer, in his terrible dilemmas or even in the outcome of his long deliberations. All I needed at that moment was for him to stand up and pull me from that booth and take me home. I needed him to restore me to everything I knew about the world and order and affection and behaving as we knew we should, even if he had to sacrifice himself.

"Well, we both believe in family. Right? That's important to us both, more than fame or riches or any selfish little pleasures...."

"Really?"

"Listen. Trust me. I'm getting there."

"Right." I was so relieved to be included on his philosophical team again that I didn't wait for the end of his sentence. "But you risked everything we had—the allowance we live on and our whole, normal family life for a house you could have anyway if you went at it right—if you went to lawyers and trustees, if you did it legally—and you didn't have to drag Maya down with you. You could go about things decently."

"Decent. Sure. Like everybody else in my family. Stop the religion. Teach English. No more hula—it's indecent. Divide up the land. No thanks. Mihana can have it. It's never been close to being mine. No taro," he went on, addressing the damp table between us. "Only plant sugar cane. Take up with the daughters then refuse to marry them. Is that decency?"

The boy with the towel put some music on, Hawaiian music, something in slack key. Paul finished the last beer in his glass and put his head back tiredly and closed his eyes. Dark lashes I had loved. "Do you remember how it was?" I said. "Paul, remember me?"

There were his hands again, wrapped tight around his glass. They held our future. I thought he had come to give it back to me. "So. School's about to start," he said uneasily, lifting his head. "There money in the bank?"

I shook my head. He knew there wasn't. He had drained our joint account. What did it matter? If he came home now our allowance from Hilton's estate would carry on.

He stared down at his glass; I stared at my empty hand. Where was the boy with the towel? I looked around fidgeting. "Didn't you order a pitcher?"

"Does she miss me?" Paul lifted his chin and the boy appeared with a pitcher and my glass. I was protected, taken care of again. Without Paul I would never be served in public places. I would have no money. Kit would get no clothes or books for school. I would be poor. I would have to work in a store, I would have to rent out our bedroom to soldiers and we would sleep on folding

190

cots; I would have to find love in bars, hang out in Waikiki; I would have to go home to Kansas to live decently. My husband was here and we hadn't talked in weeks. I cleared my throat, adjusted my skirt which was sticking to the oilcloth seat.

"Kit?"

"Maya," he said. "Is she okay? I couldn't handle it with her. I tried to send her away." His shirt, under the arms, was wet with sweat, but there was no sign of heat on his face. He looked at me solemnly.

"You mean...."

"I wouldn't be able to give you much," Paul told his beer.

"You mean...."

"I mean wherever I end up, if it's with her, even if I marry her, they're bound to cut the money off. And I don't make much on my own, do I?"

As if his hands were around my throat, I rasped, "You and Maya—you can't marry her! It's impossible! It's repulsive—the two of you!"

Paul's face froze. As if he could not bear the sight of me, would never look at me again, he closed his eyes and his face, like stone, went gray and blank.

"I hurt you," he said very quietly. "And she's very young. But she'll grow up. You don't have to be a shit. It's not the first time in history a girl fell in love with a grown man."

"Not the first time it happened at Revere either," I said.

Paul opened his eyes. He looked down at his beer as if it had made him drunk. He shook his head. The room was filling with people, strangers, soldiers. They wore black lace-up boots and brown fatigues, and they had pale, closely shaved faces and heads. Someone yelled at the bar boy. The soldiers were ordering drinks and they had taken over the jukebox so that the din in the room was growing louder and more sentimental all the time.

"Did you ever love me?" I said. "And Kit?"

191

Paul hung his head. "We're a family," he said. "At least we tried." It was country and western they were playing on the jukebox now. All that loss. I thought of a snapshot I had taken of Paul and Kit at Christmas. She had on a red dress trimmed with white, her thin arms thrown around his neck. "Kit's your child! She's your own flesh and blood!" The last photograph.

"If you want a father for her, find one then. Maybe your friend Larsen. Your overnight guest. Mr. Shin."

For a few seconds we said nothing else. Neither of us spoke.

Then I said, "He shouldn't have said.... Paul, I love you. I wish you knew that."

And he said, "It's a stone around my neck. All that love. It's a burden to me, Jess." Then he said, "I need her badly," at which he took my shoulder in his hand, pressing his fingers into it. "I'm going to talk to her. I'm leaving you."

I whispered, "No. Never. No, she's your sister. You have to believe me. She's your father's child. I mean it. Don't leave. I won't be left."

And Paul said something I couldn't hear. We were suspended in fury, only making faces, mouthing nothing. Sister. Never. Trust me. Never. Leave me.

I couldn't hear.

All I could hear was the thud of glass in my hand, and I saw a great jet of beer pour upward like a film running in reverse. The echo of that thud went through the room. The soldiers were laughing, rough-housing. They hardly turned. The beer was hurled up, hitting at air, and I somehow pulled myself out of the booth again, sideways, scraping my skin against the oilcloth. I somehow escaped, moving as fast as I could to the door, pulling it open and merging with the thick blaze of an August Hawaiian day.

From the dark bar I entered a darker world of heat and touch and smell. A world of unfamiliar faces. A world of crack seed stores and pool halls and a pizza place, where a woman in pink shorts stood languidly on the corner and a teenager drove by with a surfboard on his car. I raced by them, passing a bicycle shop, a Korean restaurant, a parking lot.

Child born of child. Lovers born of the same father. Daughter love. Sister love. I'd slipped my moorings. I had lost my mind.

And he will take Maya away. And she will go with him. And they will live among the flowers and fruits of Revere, watching their children on the lawn.

I thought of crumpling to the ground. I wanted everyone on the sidewalk to condemn Paul. But I ran on. I'd left a sandal in the bar under the table — or I had kicked it off after I left. My car was somewhere far behind me in the parking lot. Realizing that, I stopped and retraced my flight, past the Korean restaurant again, the bicycle shop, the pizza place and crack seed store. But the car was gone. Paul had taken it. I was alone.

I found myself later at a table in a dull café, holding a glass of water and my purse, the waitress kind enough to leave me there so I had time to count the years backward and sip the warm water while Paul drove the car to our house. Twelve years, traveling together, sharing the weaknesses of our pasts, the pursuits of our families, the biases of our tastes. Having our child, his child, my child, for nothing—all a waste.

ALBUM

There is a picture taken on a winter morning when my father stands on the front porch of his parents' house. The picture is in black and white. Where I come from, in the heart of the Middle West, in the middle of middle America, we are fighters. When there is war, you fight. My father holds a canvas bag and looks out at the land which billows around him like a sheet that has been shaken hard at the corners before it is tucked in. There is snow on the fields but ground shows through around the stubble underneath. Under the snow are the sunflowers that ran wild in the corn field. When the snow came they were caught, still bursting with seed. A flock of crows is feeding, circling, crying over the field and beating their wings. The men who would clear the field of sunflowers are at war in Europe or the Pacific. They are fighting and being injured, they are dying.

There is a leafless hedgeapple tree close to the porch and below that, like sentinels, two white pines. The hedgeapple is part of an old windbreak, part of a line of trees planted in rows two or three deep along rural section lines. No one knows the origin of the pines. They must have come with the pioneers. They appear in pairs marking old house sites. There are two at the old Kilmer place, a piece of empty land. Perhaps they came across the country in frail covered wagons, by twos, as if each wagon were an ark. The white pine does not reproduce in Kansas but it survives.

The porch my father stands on is already old. There is a woman near him in a dark dress in the doorway. She looks out at her grown son and at the blessing and waste of the fields. This is my grandmother, Alice Tilson, and her son is the last man in the area to leave for the war.

"You have the lunch then," she says.

He pats the bag, then drops it at his feet and turns around to pull the door open, smiling down awkwardly as cold air and light enter the dark room and touch her hair, which is pulled tightly back, and her loose skin. For a second the light is in her eyes so she is unable to look up. She is thinking, how will I ever keep the fields going, and at the same time she is pleased with her sacrifice of him. "Go on with you," she says, pulling away, having no thought that I am waiting there in his flesh, about to be conceived. Better she should have said, no, never. Don't leave. Instead she says, "Go on. Be good. Behave." It is the rule around which all Tilsons are raised.

They hear the train approach and he picks up the bag again and turns. After the years of drought and struggle, after the dustbowl and depression, she watches him escape into the early morning light that rises from the ground where corn and wheat and sunflowers are covered in autumn ice. Everything in this picture is black and white. The country my father moves through when he climbs on the train is as still as cloth, as white as milk. He does not look back at his mother or the porch. He will return in six weeks. He will have a uniform and a new wife. In a few hours he will meet my mother and they will begin my life.

My father stops in her family's hotel for the night. Her sisters warn her, as usual, about new, unknown guests. They tell her to be careful. My father stands in my mother's bedroom doorway pouring her a drink from his flask. Later he puts his mouth on hers. I am almost alive. My father offers my mother a drink.

There is a harvest moon which is large and round and orange and hangs so low it appears to be something growing out in the field. My mother is shy but she has been waiting for something all her life. She gives him her body. She bears me so I will comfort her in his absence and so I will comfort him when he comes home from the war. From the beginning, I am the only bridge from one of them to the other.

I think this is what happens. This is what makes an honest woman of my mother. A wedding ring. And he brings a gold bracelet home from the war and tells her to save it for me. My mother and I guard his house like a pair of pine trees.

Next to the picture of my father I have a picture of Hilton Quill — only one — taken on a bright midday on a beach below Revere, with a party of friends. Everything in this picture has color— the blue of the ocean, the white of the sand and the green of the grass around the house in the distance, the purple and scarlet bougainvillea dripping over a trellis, the lavender-flowered vines against the red wood.

He leaves his friends far down the beach, telling them he'll be back, and crosses the sand walking parallel to the water for a while. He extricates himself from shoes, shirt, and pants. He leaves his watch behind on the nest of clothes. He limps across the jutting trunks and interwoven branches of hau trees along the lower shore, stepping out of the stillness of the beach in 1936 and entering the jungle.

This is what he wants. This is his new boss's place but he knows Henry Needham isn't home. Hilton is moving carefully, feeling the jungle floor under his bare feet. A city boy by birth, a mainlander from Chicago, he wants absurdly to get lost in these woods, to give himself over to them, to belong to this place. This is where the North Shore woman used to live. When Needham bought this land he gave her a small parcel close to the plantation. There are politics of love and politics of sugar but she is somehow immune to them. She never touches Henry Needham but Quill is a stranger and she accepts him. She has his child.

There is life in the land, she says. In the life of the land is the preservation of righteousness. She has the eyes of a bird sailing overhead. See? she says. From every child there is some good. My child will be the vine that spreads along the shore and hugs the cliffs and travels the windward side until it comes to the place I used to live. Walk through those trees, she says. You going to raise children there. She dares him to enter the place naked, when Needham is away.

Hilton Quill scrambles across a pile of rocks. Needham's house is beyond the trees. At the edge of the jungle, close to the house, there is a large plumeria tree. He grasps a branch which snaps off in his hand and the milky sap, which causes a rash, spatters him and he curses and breaks into a sweat. He will have to go back to the sea to wash.

But Julia is in the garden. It is the garden that brings her out into the salty wind, into the smell of the sea and the man who has washed up on her shore. She is wearing a lauhala hat. At the moment of Hilton's oath, she turns from her work of clipping a vine. The hat causes shadows to play across her face. Putting a hand up to clamp down the hat, she walks into the jungle. She has heard someone call out. Without a shirt, cuffs, trousers, or hat, the person she finds looks oddly benign, part of the garden and the trees, so that she isn't frightened or embarrassed. She smiles as he holds the broken branch in front of him. Seeing that he is covered with sap she signals and turns and he follows her up the rise of ground where the house sits, its doors thrown open, its wood still dark red and new. It is a long, elegant house with a double-pitched red roof, shaded by a monkeypod and banyan trees.

Julia indicates a bath house by removing her hat and waving it at a small thatched building. The proverbial grass hut. Inside

Hilton finds a cotton robe on a peg, a faucet, and a metal bucket. The roof dribbles bugs and debris. The walls are laced-together fronds of some plant long gone brown and dry. They crackle and the staleness of the hut gives off odors that are at the same time pleasant and alarming. He wonders if this bath house is what remains of the North Shore woman's home. While he washes quickly, and pulls the length of white robe around him, belting it with its sash, Julia is on the other side of the thin wall trimming a climbing vine called deadly nightshade. She gives it a flat fan shape. She pulls the loosened branches away from the plant, clutching at some of the red berries which split and stain her hand. She has planted it in a cool, dry spot. One day, when she realizes she has helped her husband and a child walk into the open mouth of sin, she will eat a fistful of these berries and die alone in her carefully researched and planted garden. But now she licks at the stain. It spreads slightly, widening across her skin.

"Thanks for the water and robe. Have you cut yourself?"

"Not at all. I am having my first taste of poison." She smiles for the second time.

Julia's hair is straight and unpinned. She wears no powder on her face. On the way into the house she drops the hat. She thinks she has found a shore bird that needs rescuing. She wants a husband and a child, a platter and a cradle and a butter churn. The shore bird needs her and she wants to lie down beside him. "There is rain on the cliffs...do you smell it? The first drops," she says. "Come...into my house...."

This is the history of our parents—Paul's and mine. This is the way they meet. Each photograph speaks of a lost event, each picture represents reality past. But there are too many spirits in my house, too many pictures, too many women. I long for the body of one man. Husband, father. But I have no picture of my father as a father. Taken in remembrance of him. He is always a child, never old, never quite grown, he has not grown past those brief moments he spent in my mother's bed. I see him as a boy of ten at the Chautauqua beside a car, outside a tent, because I have a snapshot of him there, unfocused and wavery. I see him as a child still in 1942 when he first leaves home and meets my mother. He's twenty-four years old, desirable—almost the same age Paul was when I drove away with him. My father's well coordinated, I can see it in his hands. He's thin. He dances well. He doesn't sleep enough. I see something anxious in his eyes. He is hard to hold.

I was a daughter once, brown-haired, blue-eyed, and thin. When was I found unfit? I live in a country of comfortless women—children, mothers, spinsters, and wives. I wear a dress in which I place my hands. Scissors, paper, stone. Everyone knows that injury can be cut out. Father. Husband. You teach me a taste for you, then leave. You find other women who call you divine. But they are like me. We are ahead of you waiting in the place you journey to and we are the ones you left behind. I am Julia, my mother, and Mihana. Kit. I am Maya. I too looked for a god. I looked for a platter and a house. I looked for the resurrection of the body in a child.

TWENTY-FOUR

"Daddy was over here while you were gone!" shouted Kit. The waitress from the café where I'd been after I ran away from Paul had put me in her car and taken me home. "Auntie Mihana came in too, shaking leaves around and water, mumbling...."

"Mihana's harmless," I said dismally. "Don't let her worry you."

"I think they made up," said Kit. "Anyway Maya and her. She took Maya and all her stuff away in the truck. Anyway."

"Why do you keep saying that? 'Anyway'." Tremendous relief. They had escaped Paul. What had Mihana been doing to my house? Exorcising Maya's spirit? Paul's? Or mine? What were her powers, her dreams? Some people said she knew a curse or two.

And did it matter that the glass she held was sometimes full of gin, the offering to Pele? And did it matter that she drank it down and, as I knew, could dance the sacred hula? Who knew how much hard truth she saw? Who knew how old she was when she slept with Hilton the first time, or if her daughter had been born into her myth or from his sin?

Mihana knew enough, clearly, even if she knew Paul was coming for Maya only because he had called me from Revere.

There was my back yard, the filthy grass, the mango tree, where a cardinal swooped under the tin roof to pluck at the scarlet berries of the waving asparagus fern. The plant was dry and brittle, going yellow, dropping feathers of itself on the lanai. The whole yard was overgrown and gone to seed. In two months we had been swallowed by foliage so thick that anyone would have to hack a path through it to get us out again.

My hair had gone uncut all summer and I took it out of its barrette and ran my hand through it, shaking it out. The syrup smell of mango juice was everywhere; the egg-shaped fruit was underfoot. I stepped through it, feeling the stringy, sticky flesh between my toes.

I took my shirt off and lay back on sticky grass. Overhead the sky was blue like sea water and clear; the sun poured down its heat. I felt the mango sap and grass against my skin and my sweat starting up and dripping out of me under my arms and along my spine, then trickling noiselessly into the ground, connecting me to it, salt bond.

"Where did they go?" Each family has its myths. "Maya. Mihana. Where'd they go?"

"Auntie Mihana said, get in the truck, child, that's all."

"And?"

"Then my dad came. And he didn't even see my new radio. He just ran in and ran back out again."

Before I left to look for them, I took a journey through my daughter's room, the room where childhood was measured out and saved. It is as clear as this: her narrow bed, its headboard and footboard made of woven cane—a daybed with a comforter and matching curtains on the window under which she sleeps. Behind her head a narrow bookcase with her Oz books and a shelf of animals and two stuffed horses that we bought in San Francisco and a bear from Disneyland. The Checkers and Pogo record player. The radio. A doll house on the floor. Two rock stars on the wall behind her desk. She wants to be a singer now. Next to them, the angel with a mandolin I gave her when she had bad dreams when we lived someplace else. The angel is cherubic but her wings are red. A hanging shelf next to the desk holds all those delicate and useless gifts that people think appropriate to childhood: a painted Russian egg, an ivory tea set, four silk Chinese horses, and a mouse who reads the London *Times*. The painted yellow desk is covered with her hair bands, barrettes, and colored pens. In bowls and cups there are a dozen little pins. A box holds change. On a doll bureau near her bed are her collected hats.

And on the bed itself the yellow cat lies stretched out. His open eye, intolerant, regards me. From our positions at opposite ends of the child's bed, we consider my alternatives. Kit waits in the hall.

Now, with my eyes closed, I can see myself. Pick up the toys. Small radio, doll house, and furniture. Tea set and painted egg she saved. And bear, pick that up too. Pick up the tiny claw of spout and pinch. Pick up the bear and pull. Its leg comes off and spills an odd finality into the room. Pull down the shelf. The conscientious mouse, the Russian egg, exploding whiskers, flowers, everything. Take up the skate and fling it hard against the glass. The ruffled bed will gather up the shards. They will lie safe in pockets of the night. Like thoughts, like diaries. Hair bands and bobby pins roll under bonnets, glass, and guts of bear. Tear up the books. Take down the mirror. Take up your child's hand. And say your prayers. Behind you now, the angel beats her wings.

I set off down the road on foot, placing the diary and Mihana's stone in the deep pocket of my dress, Kit following. The sun doesn't set on this side of the island but there's a vain rose tint to things. What I had to travel were suburban streets, so I chose the longer way, turning off into the swamp, the light fading around us as we walked, Kit like a small coach pacing me, saying, "Here's the best tree," or "Don't you hate that mean dog, Mom?" along the way.

We turned left and wound past houses, breaking stride for joggers in our path. In someone's yard, a plumeria tree was covered with creamy, yellow-edged flowers. I thought of Julia. In this thick, luminous air, each object stood out as if we walked against a backdrop, as if nothing we said or did would matter very long, as if we would walk through this picture and out the other side. Our words fell into the emptiness of a darkening landscape. We began, automatically, to lower our voices and speak in whispers, as if we were moving through an alien place.

Across the road Kalaheo high school glittered. Its windows caught the falling light and flashed behind empty swings on an empty playground.

We turned off the road and into the swamp. We walked through *kiawe* and *halekoa*, through metal and thorns. And then the first small heaps of trash: old mattresses with springs and cotton bursting from confinement, parts of stoves and pieces of chairs. We passed a flowered mattress, upright against the rail, and looked away, embarrassed by the yellow stuffing, evidence of sleep and procreation behind which rolled the vast acreage of Kawanui, first landing place of the old voyagers and last estuary of the island chain. At the end of the swamp road with all its piled trash rose Mihana's old *heiau*. Far ahead of us, two or three miles away, the smell and damp of the sea.

The Lady of the Swamp was just around the curve of chainlink fence, and what I wanted was the sight of her on her tree, to come up to her on foot. See her above. Kit gripped my arm. Something had stepped into the road, into our path, as if a pile of the dark decay had just produced it. Behind, a white dog paced, wary and skeletal, and I stopped.

I had reached the first mound of broken cars, signaled by strips of cloth that fluttered from battered doors. Bits of paper, long since washed of purpose, lay scattered across the road. We stopped. Three of us and a dog: nobody moved. The apparition's squint took us in, guide and follower, without a sign of knowing who we were. She held a hand over her eyes, in a salute or in the way of people who live always in the sun.

Kit recognized her first. "Auntie!" she yelled, and waded through a deep rut in the road to reach her side. Startled, some large white egrets swung to flight above us, but I stood rooted to the earth.

"What are you doing here?" I said loudly, as if she had grown deaf. "Where's Maya anyway?" Now Kit was clinging to Mihana's hand and fastening herself to Mihana's flesh. "And what did you do to my house?"

"Only a blessing, Jesse. Some sea water sprinkled at the corners with ti-leaves. It's an old custom here when something is about to begin."

"And Maya?"

"Maya is with Paul. She's all right."

"You cannot do this," I announced. "She cannot have him. You have to prove that to them—that's why I was going there. You know it's beyond impossible—what they're doing. We're parents. Children are what matter. You know it isn't right." We heard the beat of a wing as a last egret, thin as the shivering dog, sailed out of the grass.

Kit's blond hair caught the wind. Mihana stared. Under the grass and birds and wreckage, the old *heiau* was crumbling away, slipping a few inches further from its past. The dog turned and peed against a wreck. Mihana signed to him and started leading him into the grass. She said, "She is going to have a child."

She strode along, ahead of me, massive against the sky.

The long grass, the clouds, the wheeling birds.... "What did you say?" I was running to keep up. The mud and weeds were ruining my dress.

"His child."

But what about his child by me, our child, our love? "She can't! Does she know...? Does she know her ancestry? Isn't it time you confessed?"

"The god Ku took his sister," Mihana said. "The third Kamehameha loved his sister. They would have made the highest marriage. Here, in Hawaii, the love between a brother and a sister is the best. Kamehameha's child could have saved the kingdom, but the missionaries made them ashamed. No such child's been born for a long time. This is a very special thing." She was hardly speaking to me. She was talking to the stones, the birds, the grasses, and the sky. She was speaking to her wilderness. The great mound erected to her ancestral god, a god who appeared and disappeared, rose behind her. What claim could I lay? Her long dress seemed to grow right out of the grass and swept up to cover her legs and belly and breast, leaving her great arms exposed. Tall and beautiful in flowing holoku, she had braced herself. She stood, legs far apart. She'd twisted flowers in her hair. She'd dressed up for this occasion.

"But does she understand? You have to stop her from this stupid, stupid waste!"

"Jesse! Think what you say to me!"

"Here there are twenty kinds of mischief," I reminded her. My legs were ice. My knees. "You have to tell them who her father was. Tell Paul at least. I tried. Make him believe it or he will take Revere." Maya would have equal claim on him.

A shadow moved across Mihana's face. But we were battling on her ground. "A child of such mana—it's almost inconceivable. Huh," she said mirthlessly. "Pardon the pun. She is the daughter of Captain Cook, like all of us. You listen here. We offer prayers until he comes. We build him little altars made of sticks and stones. Then when he finally comes we lie with him. Is that what you think of us? Is that what this is? Huh?

Mihana pulled a clump of grass out of the earth. "For the vital organs," she said stoutly, "you take a hatful of the stems and flowers and young shoots of the peperomia. The bark of certain roots. The roots of certain plants. So. Then no more baby. Is that what you want?" She smiled at me and rubbed a toe in the moist dirt. "It is simple to stop life. Not so difficult to put a stop to love. But improbable to make Paul come back to you," she said.

"When did you know about this?"

"Only today. I didn't hear my own thoughts in my own head. That's why she went to you. She wanted you to understand and to partake. To make this baby yours as well.... That's true, yes. Now you must give Paul and Maya their hour at least."

The house will crumble around a woman with no name, I thought. And my house will rot, will rot.

But I will give them this. This hour.

The sky was dull, and there was just the sliver of a moon. Kit stood a little way apart.

Mihana and the dog had disappeared.

TWENTY-FIVE

An hour then. Kit and I walked alone. I was an animal, injured, making its way back home. Revere was the only world I had. And the people who belonged to it. Leaving the road we climbed to the back of the YMCA, where children were playing in the fenced backyard and where the swimming pool lay long and empty. Beyond the fence, where the land was wild again, there was a sign: *Beware of Dog*. Then a few feet farther a plaque that read:

Built by the Mythical Menehunes
For the worship of the Hawaiian Gods
Its size may be estimated from the remaining terrace
Which is 140 feet wide and 30 feet high

Green and silver lichen, wild tomato plants, and climbing morning-glory vines covered the stones of the old *heiau*, but it was enormous, this platform, its corners precise, its surface still level where it had not crumbled away. The *menehunes*—the first leprechaun-like dwellers—must have passed these stones hand over hand for more than twenty miles. Each stone was the size and twice the weight of a small, very heavy child.

I dug into my pocket and brought out the small, smooth stone Mihana had given me, wrapped in its ti-leaf. "Don't put it here," Kit whined. "It's magic, isn't it?" The ti-leaf had turned paper-thin. Perhaps it was all beyond my understanding, I thought, trying to tie a new and smaller leaf around the rock, but it didn't fit and more and more the exercise began to seem absurd. I put the stone back in my pocket. Only the great trees and the wild grasses of the marsh were with us here. I stepped up on the prehistoric mound jumbled and tangled with weeds and saw a path of smaller, fitted stones that started where I stood. The stones were loose and turned underfoot. Kit was moving back toward the YMCA, backed up against the fence, worried and cross. But this was Mihana's work, I thought, she had invested herself in this. The stones were dark. They had been here much more than a thousand years. At the corner of the platform there was a steep drop. My path led down. There was a glimmer through the branches of the overhanging trees and I crawled along, descending, trying to see what it could be. An old taro patch on the right where the leaves of the plants were enormous from neglect, as if magnified by time, and behind that a corrugated tin fence bearing the painted word: *Kapu*. Keep out. Next to that there was a perfectly round, stone-lined, shallow well, as if dropped there by a god. Perfect, round, the size of the circle made by my arms, a thousand years old at least.

A bird cried *ta wher ta wher*. I found my way down the slope to the well. I touched its surface with my hand. There was a fish swimming there, about the size of a nail, a huge tree arching above. The water was only inches deep, perhaps fed by Mount Olomana farther inland. From here it trickled on into the swamp.

A small basin of fresh water. I stood over it. Dust to dust. Salt water from me to you, I said. I put my hand in the water and splashed my face. I cannot cry for anyone now or I will cry for all of us.

I thought of Paul then as if memorizing him, as if afraid that, meeting him in the hallway of Revere, I might not know him any more. I'll be wearing my dress with the deep pockets. Carrying a stone, I might have said. As if to drown myself.

I carried Paul's image and the pictures he'd made in my mind. I needed them. His arm, his face, his eyes and his voice, things I had loved. As if drowning, I rehearsed everything.

Then I climbed the great loose mound of stones again, up and up, legs wobbly, feet turning under me. At the top, I stepped off the *heiau* and signaled to Kit and we walked on through Kailua town.

I held the unwrapped stone and the old notebook, and I walked to the ancient tired house where the leaf mold and the snails and the larvae of insects and the cockroaches and lizards were the only things that stirred.

I walked into Lanikai and then along the beach, cooling my tired feet in the cold, soft waves. I went up the shore under the ironwoods, the banyan tree, passing the double-petaled hibiscus closed up and sheathed like knives, passing the fruit growing in the trees, still green and clinging to the branch.

The sky was cloudless, stretched above us like a sail. It was almost dark. There were no stars to lead us into night.

"Hey!" I called in my old Kansas voice. "Is anybody here?"

There was no sign of anyone, only a growl of thunder and heat, no sound anywhere.

If it rains we'll be safe, I thought, as if fate and the weather were syllables of a code I'd learned and forgotten, as if the code had come back to me, standing outside the long, neglected house built by Paul's grandfather and loved by Paul. Fate and the weather were things that put events like these beyond my control.

Ahead of me Kit had reached the door and now she flung it back as if ready to shout into the ears of the old house. But there was no answer.

211

"Go in," I whispered. My throat hurt. I felt like retching. I saw our car and knew Paul was there. And I wanted him—wanted him as he had always been.

We stepped inside.

There was no sense in this place any longer of who had taken and who had given pleasure or pain. Two women lived here with the vines and the jungle of trees at the back of the land, with the bufo toads that crept out on the drive at night to eat the insects under the lamps by the gate.

Maya's small things filled the place again as they had recently filled mine. There were signs of her in the hall, warm as clues left at the scene of a crime. Her comb and hair things on a table near the door, her purse, a sandal dropped, a bracelet near a wilting flower. Never had I known anyone as buoyant, as alive as this grown child. Like Paul, she'd been born into Hilton's hands. Like him, she was easy to love. But what was beautiful in Maya was youth, and youth is life itself. Looking at her, we fell in love with time stretched out ahead. It caused my tenderness and Paul's lust.

On the sills and window glass and the torn screens, small geckos clicked. The creamy, heavy smell of jasmine hung outside, thickening the night that was to come.

"Where's Daddy?" Kit said in a voice that sounded too loud for the emptiness, as if she demanded this information from the walls themselves, and not just me.

"Is there anything I should do?" she said strangely, pressing my arm with small pressures of her fingertips and palm.

I didn't answer. I was shuffling along, thinking the shallow steps ahead might weaken me, that Paul might be there waiting.

"Daddy?" cried Kit. "Where are you? Please?" She called out as if her role in our own triangle had not ended.

Now we could hear the gentle slap of the tide, methodical and urgent behind the silence of the house. I reached out for no reason, perhaps to hold the sound of it away. For a long time the

212

tide had made advances on the land. With the flat beach almost gone, the little cliff was only held there by the ironwoods.

I touched the journal that I carried in my pocket, and felt the ti-leaf with its precious cargo of charmed stone.

Then we heard the clink of the sailboat.

"Come on!" Kit urged.

"No! You stay here! I'll be back. But I want to see him alone."

I went outside. As I crossed the lawn I saw, clear as a picture, his parting at the age of nine, a pier, the grey Aloha tower reaching into the sky, girls dancing as Mihana held him against her cotton dress and Hilton started up the car and waited, motor running, for Mihana to climb in again. Mihana's hands were on his shoulders. For a minute only, they were like grown-ups saying goodbye. Aloha. Then Paul watched as she went back to his father's car.

I imagined him in those photographs of the future that would pour into yellow boxes in this house. Still walking, I looked ahead. Where would he keep them all? I tried to imagine him older, with another wife and a different child.

Oh Paul, years ago you must have known that I was putting my hair up, waiting for you in my mother's house.

I cross the wild lawn of this soiled house. The wind is coming and seems to push me along. I am tired. My feet drag. The light is failing but through the wall of ironwoods there is a sail flapping. I see a man and a young girl lying together under it. The boat is pulled up on the sand.

I grip the grass with my bare feet, walking lightly over the sharp ironwood cones that litter the scrub under the wavery trees. Their long needles look like hair unfastened in the wind. The light is failing, but through the wall of ironwoods there is the thin sound of the sail rigging against the mast.

Paul is lying with Maya on the boat, having taken her child self and the child within her to the edge of the water where they are grounded in twilight, a sail slapping softly, swinging a little above them from side to side. The fringed arms of coconut palms wave, ragged, around them and the water sucks at the boat. It washes in and out across the silvery sand. The smell down here is sullen because the wash of brine is endless and the sea along this shore has wept and retreated, wept and retreated like the people who have lived here. I can see my husband's body held in Maya's skinny, childish arms. The water washes in and out.

"Away!" I scream coming up to them. "Off the boat!"

"Jess!" This is Paul.

Maya looks up surprised. I want to take her with me to my house, to show it to her as it has been and never will be again, Paul stretching in the sunlight of the bedroom window, moving through its feathered light, my husband. And the small hallway, with its doors, and the matted room where we once lived, springing now with weeds, and the clock and teapot and butter knives and table, scene of our final discontent.

Tomorrow you will wake up intertwined, arms interlocked, as if you'd grown that way over long seasons, as if you've forgotten me, I try to say.

I want a sacrifice. For small Mihana. I want a rite. I take the round stone out of my pocket with its bandage of dead leaf and roll this offering, the first I have, into the sea.

Perhaps Mihana, in her room, is moving overhead. She paces back and forth, between the window and the desk. She washes her hands, shakes out her hair, and puts her plain dress on. Then she sits at her broken desk and rummages through the papers she keeps there, thinking of an old book she's lost, drumming her fingers on the battered wood.

"Away!" I shout again.

Paul leaps up. Maya tumbles off. Paul pushes the boat into the sea but I climb on.

Paul comes in after me. "You don't know how to steer, Jess!" I'm on the boat but he is coming through the water, grabbing the bar across the two hulls at the stern. "Jess, you don't know how. Let me on!" I hold the tiller and we are swept out to the open water. "Shit, Jess, drop the sail!" he warns. "Let me up or you'll go over...," he yells. "What the hell? We don't have to do this! Just love me enough to let me...go.... That's proof...of love...listen...." He's being pulled now, but there is too much between us, too much space.

"She's your sister," I scream back at him. "Your father's child. Go on. Let go. I can't stop. Go back to her."

"Don't be stupid! I don't care who she is! Jess...let me on, let me help." He is struggling, kicking. "Can't you give up?" he shouts. "Can't I take care of my own child?"

The two islands are lovely as we sail past them, Paul hanging on. His arm is bruised in the gray light but I do not stop to take him on board. There is no sunset here. No lingering blaze. On this side of the island there is the sudden clap of night when the sun falls behind the Koolaus.

"Jess!" Feeling the growing wind. "Bear off if you can.... Jess! Please. Listen. That's the only way to get back in, Jess!"

I drop the tiller and put my hand inside my dress and pull the journal out and climb up on my knees, causing the boat to swing and tip, the delicate brown scrawl to disappear in the sea air, but I can no longer think of that. The words are almost gone. My hair is blowing, beating at my face. From somewhere there is a strong, hard wind. We are far, far from land. "Paul, look. Paul, I have proof of everything I said. At Pinky's. I have it right here...." My eyes are stone.

This is the second offering.

Maya is watching from the shore. Kit has run down to her from the house, even Mihana may be there standing above the water and the trees. But the old journal with its mutterings is nourishing my hands and arms.

I wonder if none of this is true. If Mihana wants me to believe she is Paul's sister. And to believe that Maya is Paul's sister too and that she's carrying a child by him. Perhaps it is a trick, a terrible way to rid herself of him.

"Here," I say again. I strike the book hard, hard against his hand. The words, all the words are gone. Even the photographs I carry in my mind. All our pictures, our past. Nothing of us is left. Paul grabs at the book, losing hold of the bar. I pry the fingers of his other hand off, then I release him and, without his weight, the boat lurches and tips and leaps across the silver water.

"Jess!...You know I can't get back!"

I think of Paul's thin face in the dark, tasting of salt. I think of his eyes and his cheekbones. I think of the hollows in his neck and dark angles of his mouth. I think of his sex, too, which tastes of brine, and of his child, who is the fruit of it, the heat of his body entering mine.

"Jess, give me your hand...." He reaches up but he is no longer my own. He is already lost. In the sudden darkness, I can't see him, I can't steer the boat well enough, but I hear him calling me.

"Love," I say.

The boat swings and turns. I see his arms for the last time. They are churning the darkening sea. Body I've loved. My bitter heart. The wind picks up and the boat sweeps past him and away.

TWENTY-SIX

I used to lie in bed and watch the mango leaves beyond my bedroom wall. Watch dark leaves drying after a quick rain, reflecting sunlight, swaying, brushing on the overhang of roof. I saw the tree from underneath then, looking up to branches that were several inches thick and spread open like a hand waiting for a gift. From that angle it did not look tropical at all. Except that, when they fell, the leaves were green.

The past has four letters. Past is a four-letter word. Parts of it disappear. Like loops of gold too heavy to float, pieces of it slip below the surface and lie out of reach. My mother once threw a bracelet into the brook that flowed through our dusty yard. My father had built this brook that began nowhere and ended nowhere. He had brought the bracelet to her after the war. Maybe my mother thought she could retrieve it later, coated with buried rotten leaves and slime. Maybe she made her point. She must have regretted the action many times and gone out in her nightclothes late at night when we couldn't see her to scoop up the leaves and sort through them. But the yard and the house itself rested on a shifting, liquid foundation, and the band of gold a little larger than her wrist had disappeared, our only heirloom, never to be passed down to me. I waited, through my childhood, for something to reach out of the brook and give it back. But gold is even heavier than flesh. Words wash away. Pictures decay. All we can trust is faulty memory.

Later there was another yard, a garden, another loss. There is a place and a time for certain plants, there are nights with moons and nights without. There is power in chants. And maybe there is that hand somewhere that will push all the lost charms, all the heavy bodies back into the drawers and boxes, the secret and safe places they used to be.

But I've made arrangements. The child, the man and woman, the flowers and wild things in the garden will be memories. I will sift them like leaves. Even the cat and even the songs we sang in the car as we drove into the valleys. Even the wind and rain.

ABOUT THE AUTHOR

Linda Spalding is the author of *The Paper Wife*, also published by The Ecco Press, and the editor of *Brick: A Literary Journal*. Born in Kansas, she lived for many years in Hawaii, and now lives in Toronto with Michael Ondaatje and her cat and their dog.